THE ~~SP~~ ~~R~~

[

a ~~...~~ ~~es~~

KEVIN WOOD

Copyright © 2022 Kevin Wood

All rights reserved. The author asserts the moral right under the Copyright, Designs and Patents Act 1988 to be identified as the author of this work. No part of this publication may be reproduced, stored in a retrieval system, or transmitted, in any form or by any means without the prior written consent of the author, nor be otherwise circulated in any form or binding or cover other than that in which it is published and without a similar condition being imposed on the subsequent purchaser.

ISBN: 9798367591903

1	The Search for Ellie Babble	1
2	The Nightmare	32
3	Nemesis	43
4	When Love Dies	61
5	The Darkest Star	82
6	The Dance of Death	99
7	The Witch's Daughter	115
8	Road to Redemption	143

With thanks to Wendy Ogilvie and Paul Burridge for their expertise in bringing this book to publication. And to all my friends who inspired so me so much over the years.

The Search for Ellie Babble

In memory of Barry the Cat

1

As Ellie left Bar Q that night none of her friends realised that it would be the last time that they would see her. None of them could have imagined, as Ellie waved back to them blowing a furtive kiss in their direction, what the future had in store for them and, more particularly, for Ellie. They watched on as she opened the door to the street beyond. It revealed a dismal drizzly night. Two doormen hovered threateningly and one or two smokers puffed away on their cigarettes whilst sheltering as best they could from the damp weather. The door shut and Ellie disappeared into the night.

Ellie's friends began to finish their drinks for the evening before making their own way home. As they did so, Sonya returned from behind the bar. Sonya was a bar assistant at Bar Q but, although it was her night off, the bar manager had been discussing her working hours for the coming weekend. It distracted her enough so that she didn't notice Ellie leave.

'Has Ellie gone?' she enquired as she returned to the others at the table. They nodded. She peered outside through a nearby window. 'Looks like the taxi has gone as well,' she said, before rummaging through her small clutch bag, picking out her mobile phone so she could arrange for another one to take her home.

The Bar Manager, Ronnie, called over, 'Everything alright, Sonya?'

'It's OK, Ronnie. My friend has already left. I'm just going to arrange to get another lift home—'

Ronnie interrupted her. 'No need, Sonya. Lucy here is on her way home she can give you a lift in her car.'

Lucy was a colleague of Sonya's at Bar Q. She was ready and heading towards the door. She beckoned Sonya to join her.

At the table where Ellie and Sonya had been sitting, the others sat there were now on their feet. Two of them, Dick and his wife, were ready to go. They were waiting for the only other person with them, Maggie. They were to give her a lift home. Maggie was slightly less organised and still finishing her drink and needed to put on her brightly coloured jacket before she would be ready for them. Maggie was often one of the last to leave and as Dick had worked with her now for a number of years, he was unsurprised by her not being rushed by either their impatience or the approaching bar staff.

Maggie was still not ready as Sonya began making her way to the door. She took a long route around the bar to ensure that she was able to say goodbye to the regulars, some of whom were still drinking. Some were treated to just a cheery wave, others a peck on the cheek and some a hug as well. Maggie gave her a hug and as Sonya approached the door, Dick and his wife were already there still waiting for Maggie. Sonya gave them both a hug and peck on the cheek. Then reaching the door, walked out into the street with Lucy and they both headed off together.

At last Maggie was ready. She joined Dick and his wife by the door and they began to stroll up the street to Dick's car. It was a relatively short walk and after a few minutes they arrived at the vehicle and climbed inside.

Finally, they drove off into the night and left behind the bar now almost empty as the final customers left and the staff finished clearing and tidying. For Dick and Maggie tomorrow would be another working day.

2

Maggie arrived at work mid-morning following yesterday's late night and a couple of work queries she had received a little earlier before arriving at her desk. Her work colleagues greeted her and she began to catch up on the news of the day. Her work involved liaising with the police on behavioural problems in the community. The first item on her agenda, once she opened her e-mails, was to check if she had received any important messages overnight. Nothing too major had happened since yesterday. Although, a colleague had sent some intelligence that the police had been kept busy sorting out issues arising between local gangs. It had occurred her, and no doubt to others, that drugs were probably involved but they were not required to take an active role in any of these issues at the moment as the police were dealing with it. She noted and diarised the reports and continued with the routine of the day.

After grabbing a cup of coffee and settling down into her usual routine, she remembered Ellie had spoken to her last night about something she wanted to discuss with her. It was all a little mysterious. She decided to head over to Ellie's desk. It was in another part of the building so she grabbed her coffee and made her way to find out what the mystery was all about.

As she arrived in the office, she was greeted by Ellie's boss. 'Hi Mags. Have you seen Ellie today?' he asked.

Maggie was a little taken aback. 'No. Where is she?' Then after a pause. 'I haven't seen her since last night.'

'She's not come in this morning. We are a little concerned about her at the moment because no one seems to know where she is.'

'Dick was with us last night. Has he heard anything?' Maggie turned to look down the office towards the desk where Dick worked. He wasn't there.

'Oh. He was in earlier but went out on site visits. That was before we expected her in. So, he's probably not aware of anything at this end.'

Maggie was trying to take all this information in and process her thoughts. She shook her head. 'I've no idea. I thought she'd be here too. Was she definitely due in this morning?'

'Yes. I've no idea where she is.'

'Hang on, I'll give her call.' Maggie reached down to take her phone out of her handbag.

'We've already called her. But there's no answer. By all means see if you might have any better luck.'

Maggie listened as the phone rang. Then a recorded message intervened.

'It's gone to voicemail.'

'That's what we got too.'

'I'll call Dick and see if he knows anything about where she might be.'

'OK.'

Maggie called Dick's number.

Dick was out on house visits so it took a short while before he answered the call.

'Hi Mags.'

'Hi Dick. Have you heard anything from Ellie this morning? I've just got into the office and there's no sign of her here.'

'I see your time keeping is up to its usual standard,' Dick joked.

Maggie shrugged off his comment. 'People are getting quite worried about her. Have you heard from her since last night?' She persevered with her questioning.

Maggie noticed Dick's tone changed as he heard the concern in her voice. 'Not since last night,' he said. 'Why? What's happened?'

'She's not turned up for work this morning. I thought she wanted to speak to me about something important. That's what she said last night. And everyone here in the office was definitely expecting her in. Where is she?'

There was a silence. It seemed to last longer than

was normal. Maggie was just about to speak when Dick finally responded.

'Tell you what, Mags,' he said. 'I'm not far away from Ellie's. Do you want me to pop round and check to see if she's home?'

'Would you mind? It would be a great relief to find out she's just overslept.'

'Fine. I'm on my way.'

They both hung up.

In the office, Maggie turned back to Ellie's boss. 'Dick's going to pop round her flat and see if she's there.'

Ellie's boss nodded. 'I think HR may be checking that sort of thing out with her relatives, Still I'm sure it won't hurt to give it a try.'

It took Dick just a few minutes to drive the short distance to Ellie's flat. As he pulled up, he looked over towards the building. Although Ellie lived on the first floor, the building looked very quiet with no obvious sign of anyone being in either of the two flats. He stepped out of his car with trepidation, not entirely sure what might have happened or what he was about to encounter there.

He had taken barely a few steps down the path towards the building when a woman's voice called his name from further down the street. It was Ellie's friend, Sonya.

'Hi ... Hello. It's Dick, isn't it?' she called out as she approached him.

'Yeah.'

'Are you heading up to Ellie's?'

Dick stared up towards the building again. 'Yes. Why have you seen her?'

'Not since last night,' Sonya replied. 'Her aunt just rang me. Apparently, she had had Ellie's work on the phone because Ellie hadn't turned up to work this morning and they were concerned about her.'

'Yes, I know. Someone just called me too. It was Maggie. Do you remember her from last night?'

'Oh yeah. The one with the brightly coloured hair.' Sonya also looked up at the building. 'Ellie's aunt called me because Ellie gave me a spare key in case of emergencies.'

'Shall we go up together then?' Dick said pointing towards the flat.

Sonya nodded and started off towards the main door at the front. Dick followed. She opened the door with one of her keys and then turned towards a flight of stairs to her right-hand side. She began to climb them with Dick following just a few steps behind her. At the top of the stairs, she reached a small landing with Ellie's front door on the left-hand side. She walked past a couple of flower pots, a gnome and other garden ornaments which decorated the floor of the landing and stopped at the front door.

As Dick arrived at the top and stepped towards her, Sonya turned towards him and held out the door key hesitantly saying, 'Will ... you ...?' Dick smiled weakly and understood. The concern etched on Sonya's face gave away her worry about what might be waiting for them inside. It had stopped her in her tracks. Dick took the key out of her hand and reached for the lock on the door.

The key turned in the lock and as Dick pushed the door it cracked open and a ginger and white cat hared out and scampered down the stairs. It startled both of them. After a moment, Sonya regained her composure a little and said, 'It's OK. It's only Charlie. He's one of Ellie's cats.'

'One of them!' said Dick shocked. 'How many has she got then?'

'Only two. Molly's probably inside somewhere.'

Dick pushed the door open further and walked into a small hallway. 'Ellie,' he called out. He spotted a cat litter tray to one side of the door. In front of him there was another door that was slightly ajar. He pushed it open and walked in to what appeared to be the main living area. 'Ellie,' he called again.

Sonya was just behind him and looking around as they walked on. She gave him a nudge, pointing towards the bedroom. 'You'd better check in there, Dick. It's her bedroom.' Dick nodded and made his way back past her towards the door she had indicated. He opened it slowly and peered into the room. It was empty.

'She's not here either.'

He moved back into the main part of the flat whilst Sonya went into the bedroom. It was becoming obvious that no one was there. Sonya re-joined him inside the front room. 'Dick. There is something.'

'What's up. What have you found?'

'Nothing really,' Sonya said quietly, 'but you know the black shoulder bag she had with her last night?' Dick looked back at her quizzically. 'It's not here. I can't see it anywhere.'

'You think she's not been home since last night?'

'It looks like it.' Sonya turned and stopped as something caught her eye on the floor underneath a small wooden storage cabinet. She stooped down to see a small pair of eyes peering back from a little furry object. It was Molly. Sonya smiled weakly and gently spoke to the terrified cat. 'Hello Molly. Do you need a cuddle, babe?' The cat remained unmoved. Dick bent down to see what Sonya had found. Sonya picked Molly up. The cat was trembling but Sonya began stroking it to try and calm it down. She looked back up to Dick. 'This is Molly.' She looked back down to her. 'Are you OK babe?' As she stroked Molly, she realised the cats hadn't been fed. 'I'd better sort out some food and drink for the cats.' Dick smiled and nodded. Sonya left the room and went into the kitchen at the rear.

Dick decided he'd better let Maggie know what had happened. He rang her.

'Hi Mags. It's Dick.'

'Hi. Any news?'

'Yes. I bumped into Ellie's neighbour, Sonya. Do you remember her from last night?'

'Yes. OK.'

'We've both looked around Ellie's flat. It's empty. Sonya thinks she may not have returned home last night because her shoulder bag's not here.' The was a short pause. Maggie remained silent. Dick continued. 'Her cats are both here but they seem a little bit spooked. Sonya's sorting some food out for them.' At this point Sonya returned with a container and some food.

Maggie finally responded. 'Oh, I see.' The tone of her voice betrayed her concern. 'That's all a little worrying. Does Sonya have any idea what might have happened?'

'No. I don't think she has any more idea than we have to be honest.'

Sonya had returned from the kitchen and brought a saucer of milk back with her.

'See what else you can find out Dick,' Maggie said, still sounding noticeably concerned.

'Will do.' Dick replied. They hung up. Dick looked around the room. Despite Maggie's concern there didn't seem to be anything further he could do. He turned back to Sonya who was stroking Molly again. 'I think I may as well go. Unless there's anything more you need me to do to help?'

Sonya shook her head. 'Don't worry, I'll lock up here and check things out until Ellie comes back.'

'OK.'

3

Sonya made her way over to Ellie's flat around mid-morning the following day. It was Saturday and she was due to do a short afternoon shift at Bar Q but decided to check in on the cats beforehand to make sure they were fed and watered.

As she opened the door, she noticed some paperwork on the floor by the bedroom that hadn't been there yesterday. Charlie was prowling around the landing. She went into the kitchen and picked up the cat food and a container to put it in. Then as she made her way back past Charlie into the front room, she was shocked as she noticed the state of it. The room looked like it had been ransacked. She looked accusingly at Charlie 'Did you do this, Charlie?' The cat continued about its way oblivious to her question concentrating more on the prospect of the food she was carrying.

Looking closer, Sonya felt it looked more like someone had been in the flat and rummaged through most of the drawers and cupboards in the room. More paperwork was on the floor and a couple of drawers had been pulled out of their settings. As she emptied out the contents of the cat food into the container, Molly appeared alongside Charlie anticipating the pending feast. Sonya stopped and turned again to survey the mess. It dawned on her that someone had been in the flat. Briefly, she considered that perhaps Ellie had returned. Whoever it was must have had a key. But it looked more like the front room had been searched in a more malicious way than she would have expected from Ellie.

Had there been a break-in?

She decided to finish dealing with the cats' needs first. She got them some drink, checked the litter tray and then started trying to tidy up some of the mess. Once the room looked a bit more respectable, she left. In her mind she was conflicted about whether to report the incident but decided against it because she thought the cats may have been partly responsible. Perhaps Ellie had come back and gone again and she couldn't really be sure about anything. It was playing on her mind but she decided to wait and see if anything else happened before she took it further. If Ellie would only re-emerge it would solve everything.

Saturday morning was almost over when Maggie's phone rang. It was Dick. She was a little startled he didn't usually call on non-work days. However, events over the past day or two meant she'd already understood that these were unusual times.

'Hi Dick. How's things?'

'Hi Mags. I was just talking with my wife and we were wondering if you'd heard anything more about Ellie. I guess she's not turned up yet, has she?'

'Oh. Erm ... no I haven't heard anything since yesterday.' Maggie was at home and preparing to meet up with friends for lunch. She checked her watch. 'I could call someone see if anything has turned up. I've not heard from any of my police work colleagues at all.'

'Do you know if they're planning to contact any of us? We were just thinking that if she did vanish straight after she left us the other night, they may want to question us.'

'It's possible,' Maggie said. 'Let me make a few calls and I'll see if I can find out if there's any news.'

'OK. Call me back when you can.'

It was late afternoon when Sonya arrived at Bar Q for her shift. As she prepared to start Ronnie came over to her. 'Hi Ronnie,' she greeted him cheerfully.

'Hello Sonya. Can I ask a favour of you?'

Sonya turned towards him 'What is it?'

'Lucy is taking a few days off. Could you fill in for her shift tomorrow evening?'

Sonya paused for a moment to think and then said, 'Yeah. No problem. Is she OK?'

'Thanks.'

'Has she phoned in sick then?'

Ronnie seemed slightly irritated by the question as he turned to walk away. He turned back. 'She's taking a few days off that's all,' he said and moved back towards the bar area. Sonya stared after him and shrugged it off following him shortly after to start her shift.

A few hours had passed; the bar being fairly quiet, she decided to take her break that was already overdue. 'Ronnie,' she called over to him, 'Is it OK to take my fifteen-minute break now whilst it's quiet. Before the next rush?'

Ronnie looked around and nodded. 'Sure. Go ahead.'

Stepping outside for a few minutes, it occurred to Sonya that it would be a good time to call Lucy to see if she was OK. She picked up her phone and called her. It rang several times then stopped. Sonya paused waiting for a reply then said 'Lucy are you there?'

'Who's that?' came the response.

'It's only Sonya over at Bar Q.' Sonya recognised Lucy's voice although her tone seemed a little curt. 'I just phoned to see if you were OK.'

'Why what's happened now?'

'Nothing babes. Ronnie's told me you were going to be off for a few days. I just wondered if you were OK.' Sonya said a little surprised by Lucy's tone.

'Oh right. No, I'm fine. As Ronnie said I'm not coming in for two or three days.'

'As long as you're OK.' Sonya felt Lucy didn't seem to be herself as if something was on her mind. She seemed distracted.

'I'm fine,' Lucy said. 'You didn't need to call. I'll be back in a little while.'

Sonya was still worried about the way she was speaking, she continued. 'Are you sure everything's OK?' It was to no avail as the line had gone dead as Lucy had ended the call.

Sonya stared at the phone somewhat confused by the abruptness at the end of the conversation. After a few moments she reassured herself, at least Lucy was responding and put her curt tone down to the fact she'd probably interrupted her whilst she was busy and that had annoyed her. She checked the time and decided to get back to the bar, her break was almost over and a group of people were waiting to be served. She returned to work and continued the remainder of her shift.

4

The following day was a Sunday. It was around 10.30 in the morning when Ronnie concluded his phone call. The clouds were already gathering and he knew exactly what he had to do next. He had to leave. He had to leave the country. He had to act fast. He grabbed a suitcase and began packing. He was packing for a long time away. It didn't take too long but he was in a rush. Whilst still finishing his packing he called a trusted taxi company and they turned up promptly. He loaded his baggage into the car and then himself. Very quickly they were on the way to the airport.

A few things needed tidying up on the way. He needed to sort out things at Bar Q. He must phone one of his assistant managers. He chose Sandy. He called her and the phone rang and eventually went onto voicemail. He hung up. He needed to speak to someone directly. Pausing for a moment, he called Sue, the other assistant manager. She answered promptly.

'Morning Ronnie,' she said cheerfully.

His voice was stern. 'Sue, I need a favour from you.'

'Sure Ronnie. What's up?'

'Something has come up and I'm going to be away

for a while. Can you sort out a roster with Sandy to cover whilst I'm away?'

'Yeah. Of course. Is there anything we can help with?'

'No. Just sort things out at Bar Q. That'll be fine. Get in touch with Sandy and I'm sure you'll be able to deal with it between the two of you.'

Ronnie went on and they discussed staffing. Lucy was off for a few days. Sonya was covering the evening shift for her and other staff would be available and so on.

When he finished, Sue chipped in, 'How long are likely to be away for, Ronnie?'

'Look I'll have to go we're arriving at the airport. I'll be in touch.' The line went dead.

Sue paused to take in the information she had just received. She checked the time. Bar Q would need to be opened soon. She walked over to a nearby cabinet and picked up the keys for the bar.

Across town, Maggie had spent the previous night partying with friends at a local Irish bar, so although she had been up for an hour or two, she was still a little delicate and hadn't really taken a lot of time to gather her thoughts. Then she remembered Dick's phone call the day before and realised she ought to check in with one of her friends at the local police station to see if anything had happened that they could share with her and whether they were looking to speak to any of them about Ellie's disappearance. She called them and after a short conversation decided to relate what she could to Dick.

She called him and he answered promptly. 'Hi,' she said. 'Sorry I didn't get back to you yesterday but I've been a little busy.'

Dick laughed. 'Busy on a Saturday night! How many drinks constitutes busy?'

Maggie laughed too.

'I've found out a little more about Ellie, Dick. It's not much though.'

'Oh. What's happened?'

'Well, Ellie wasn't officially reported missing until yesterday. I think her aunt phoned it in. So, you can understand not much has happened at all.'

Dick agreed.

'I think the police are assuming she'll turn up soon anyway and, in which case, everything will sort itself out then.'

'I hope so,' Dick said, not exactly convinced.

'Anyway, as far as we're concerned, I don't expect anything much will happen until next week. They probably won't process any initial information from the missing person's report until tomorrow anyway. I think we should be just hoping for the best and waiting for anything to develop in the next few days.'

'Sounds reasonable, Mags,' Dick said. 'Perhaps we'll find out some more soon. I can't help but worry about her though. After all nobody's heard anything from her since Thursday evening.'

'Yes, I know. It doesn't sound great, does it?' Maggie replied. 'I'm hoping she'll turn up and explain what on earth happened. Perhaps she'll turn up at work tomorrow.'

'I hope so. I'll see you at work tomorrow then.'

'Yeah. See you then.'

They both hung up.

Sonya arrived at Bar Q that evening and was a little taken aback to find Sandy there instead of Ronnie. 'Hi Sandy,' she said, 'what's happened to Ronnie? I thought he was on this evening.'

Sandy smiled and brushed back her black and silver tinted shoulder length hair. 'I know, Sonya. I thought that as well. I thought I'd be sitting at home watching some trash TV tonight. Sue phoned me earlier and told me Ronnie had phoned her and left us both in charge. He's gone away or something. It's all a bit mysterious.'

'Where's he gone?'

'I've absolutely no idea! Completely out of the blue! And then I come in to take over from Sue and she tells me about Lucy's flat. It's like the world's gone crazy.'

Sonya was taking all this in but mention of Lucy reminded her of the strange phone call she had with her the day before. 'What's happened to Lucy's flat?'

Sandy was cleaning the bar counter down as she spoke. She looked quizzically at Sonya. 'I thought you knew! Isn't that why you're covering her shift this evening?'

'No. Ronnie asked me to cover for her yesterday because Lucy had told him she was taking some days off. I didn't know anything about her leaving because of her flat.'

'Yesterday?' Sandy said puzzled, 'No that can't be right. Lucy's flat was burgled last night. Apparently, completely trashed. Everything turned over. But that was last night.'

Sonya looked confused.

Sandy continued, 'Sounds like yet another mystery!'

'I don't understand what's going on, Sandy.' Sonya's mood had changed as she took in this news. 'First, last Thursday, my friend Ellie disappears. Then yesterday, I discover her flat might have been broken into as well. Now Lucy and Ronnie vanish, Lucy's flat's burgled and ...' Her voice trailed off.

'Cheer up, Sonya.' Sandy smiled and gave her a little hug. 'Tell you what we'll have a few drinks after we've cleared up tonight to give us all a bit of a lift.'

Sonya smiled back weakly and nodded.

Sandy moved away into the main bar. 'Meantime we'd best get on. These drinks won't serve themselves.'

Sonya nodded again. 'No problem, Sandy. I'm sure it'll be fine. I'll keep smiling through.' They both smiled and got back to work.

Later, in Bar Q as the evening was drawing on. Sonya was busying herself collecting empty glasses and tidying up tables. She moved around the bar near to where two young regulars, Joe and Kay, were sitting.

'Hi Sonya. You're not your usual chirpy self today,' Joe said as she passed nearby.

Somewhat startled, Sonya jumped back a little. 'Oh, hi Joe, Kay. Sorry darling I'm in a bit of a daze, my best friend went missing from here a few nights back.'

'Sorry to hear that babe,' Kay said.

'You might know my friend. Ellie? She often meets me in here.'

'The pretty girl with the long dark hair,' Joe said as Kay stared slightly reproachfully at him.

'That sounds like her.'

'What happened?' Joe took up the conversation.

Sonya grimaced a little. 'To be honest I'm a bit choked up about it. She disappeared from here a few nights back. I should have gone with her. But she disappeared.'

'I'm sure she's fine,' Kay said comfortingly.

'She's probably just having a break for a few days

somewhere or something like that,' Joe added.

'She'll turn up soon,' Kay said sympathetically. 'We all need a bit of peace and quiet sometimes.'

'I'm not so sure. She's disappeared completely.' Sonya looked downcast. 'I'm getting really concerned for her. It seems things are getting really dark at the moment. And in the back of my mind ...' She paused becoming a little emotional in her voice. 'I fear that something awful has happened to her.'

She regained her composure and looked over to the bar. 'Oh, sorry babes. There's someone waiting.' She pointed at a customer standing patiently at the bar. 'Thanks Joe, Kay. I'll catch up with you later.' She scuttled off towards the waiting customer. Joe and Kay exchanged glances and returned to their own conversation.

After the shift finished, Sonya, Sandy and the other staff had the little get together Sandy had suggested earlier. Once they wound it up Sonya called a taxi and headed for home. It was a fairly short journey but gave her a few minutes to gather her thoughts about the recent events. It wasn't too long for her to dwell on them before the taxi arrived at her street.

As they rounded the corner a little way down the road there was a commotion of people and vehicles. The taxi came to a halt. Ahead of them a building was ablaze, fire engines and other service vehicles were dotted around on the road along with a growing number of onlookers. Sonya sat still as if frozen in her seat staring blankly at the scene barely believing what she was seeing. The fire was in Ellie's flat.

Her eyes widened as she filled with panic.

Sonya flung the car door open and leapt out running towards where the crowds had gathered. 'Ellie!' she screamed somewhat pointlessly. And again 'Ellie! Ellie! Ellie! ...'

One of her neighbours spotted her and grabbed her as she ran towards them. 'It's OK. Ellie's not there. Everybody's safe.' The neighbour comforted Sonya.

Sonya completely broke down and sobbed uncontrollably in the neighbour's embrace. A couple of other neighbours came over and joined their hug.

'Ellie, I'm so sorry,' Sonya said quietly as she stared up at the burning flat and whimpered whilst the first neighbour patted her head comfortingly.

At this point Ellie's cat, Molly strolled up and began rubbing herself against Sonya's right leg as if trying to join in the hug. Sonya didn't notice. Molly looked distinctly spooked and somewhat bedraggled.

'It's OK, Sonya. Ellie wasn't in. Everyone's OK.' The neighbour repeated still stroking Sonya's head.

It was hopeless. She was inconsolable. She looked back up towards the burning building tears streaming down her face. Ellie's other cat, Charlie, was standing in front of the flat as the fire services buzzed around. The acrid smoke billowed up occasionally from the building. The cat seemed entranced by the flames as the building burned. Sonya was oblivious to all this. One of the neighbours brought her a cup of tea to try and settle her. She refused it at first, then eventually gathered herself a little and took a sip from the cup. It really didn't seem to help that much grateful though she was for the thoughtfulness of the neighbour and the taste of the drink mixed with the smoke which she had breathed in to her mouth.

The tears continued.

As time passed, the fire was being brought under control and the flames almost completely extinguished. Sonya had been led away to a neighbour's kitchen to finish her tea and with one or two other neighbours to share some words of comfort and understanding.

Eventually, Sonya was a little calmer. She was already on her second cup of tea. Molly had sat in her lap as she tried to make sense of everything that had happened.

A fire officer came to the door. The fire was out. 'Is the lady here who lives in the flat opposite?' he asked from the door of the neighbour's house. She looked around at Sonya.

Sonya got to her feet shedding Molly to the floor at the same time. 'I'm her friend,' she said weakly. 'I have been looking after the flat whilst she was away.' She was beginning to choke up again. The neighbour comfortingly touched her arm and smiled.

'OK,' the fire officer said. 'Can I have a word with you? I need a few details and you may have some questions.' Sonya stared at him uncertainly. Then composed herself a little and took a deep breath, drank down the rest of her tea.

'We'll go back to my place.' She started towards the door.

'I can come along if it's any help,' the neighbour chipped in.

Sonya thought for a moment. 'Sure. Just for a little while. It might be helpful.'

So, she marched out of the house and towards her own home. The neighbour was walking just behind her with Molly in close pursuit. The fire officer followed. Charlie spotted the procession and tagged along behind the fire officer.

As Sonya turned to her front door, she noticed in the distance on the horizon the first glow of dawn was showing through the darkness of the night, although sunrise was still a little way off. She went inside and the others followed.

5

Maggie woke up to a brand-new day. But this wasn't just any old day. This was the first day of the working week. She let out a deep sigh as that thought sank in and turned to check what the time was on her bedside clock. She was already running late. Another sigh.

As she began to get herself ready, she tidied up around the room. A task which really meant nothing more than throwing a few items of clothing once strewn around into a less dishevelled pile in the corner. Whilst placing one or two of the dirtier clothes in the laundry basket in another corner.

She then turned her mind to the day ahead. She remembered that she had a meeting planned between representatives from the local police and her colleagues. It was known as a Partnership meeting. It was a regular monthly meeting and if she had remembered correctly, the main topic on today's agenda was concerning the increasing drug problem in the area. She decided she ought to wear something a little smarter than her usual casual attire as it would be more appropriate for such a meeting. Best to leave the low-cut top at home today she thought as she chuckled quietly to herself.

Once she was ready to face the day, she checked herself in the mirror, made sure that everything was in the right place and turned to pick up her keys.

As she did so, she noticed something odd from the corner of her eye. There was a dark shape rested up against the glass at the bottom of the front door. Although slightly startled it was not especially unusual as the next-door neighbour's cat would often curl up in her doorway for a nap. This looked different. It looked larger than the usual silhouette she would have expected for the cat. And something about it seemed concerning and made her anxious as she moved slowly over and began to open the door.

Dick had already arrived in the works car park and was just about to head inside from his car and into the office when his phone rang.

It was Maggie.

He barely had a chance to answer it with his usual 'Hi Mags' greeting when he was cut short by Maggie's frantic, largely incoherent and screeching stream of desperate and emotional sentences.

'Mags. Try to calm down,' he said struggling to make himself heard over Maggie's garbled words. He persevered trying to make some semblance of something understandable from what she seemed to be saying. 'Did you say you found something?' A pause.

'What did you say? Slow down a bit. Are you OK?' Another pause. 'Where are you, Mags? What did you say? A dead body! Mags where are you?' Another pause. She was at her home. 'Stay there, Mags. I'm coming over.' Then as if to further emphasise his message. 'Mags, just stay where you are.'

The call ended and he leapt back into his car and drove off heading across town to where Maggie lived.

By the time he had reached the road where Maggie's flat was, he had been going through in his mind what could have happened and what he might be confronted with when he arrived at the incident. It was quite a long distance to Maggie's flat and as he drove along, he could hear what sounded like a police siren. It seemed to be still quite a long way off and as far as he could tell some way behind him.

As he approached a little closer, he could make out an ambulance parked up at the front of the flat and a group of people gathered on the pavement. He pulled up and parked as close as he could get given the commotion ahead of him. He slowly got out of his car and tried to take in what was happening around him. He looked over towards Maggie's front door. There was a number of people huddled together around what looked like it could be a body. He looked closer. They were paramedics. The sound of the police siren was much closer now. He looked over towards another group of people and spotted

Maggie standing amongst another huddle on the pavement about thirty yards in front of him. As he spotted her, she also spotted him.

'Dick!' she screamed and began running over to where he was standing. She threw her arms around him and began sobbing again.

'Maggie? Are you OK?' Dick said as they both hugged. 'What's going on? What's happened?'

Maggie picked her head up from Dick's shoulders and lifted her tear-filled, reddened eyes up to meet his gaze. Her face was full of emotion as she met his eyes and a tear trickled down her right cheek. She sniffed a little and quietly spoke.

'She's dead, Dick ... She's dead ...'

Dick guessed who she meant but caught up in the moment and without processing Maggie's words fully, automatically responded 'Who is?'

Maggie paused before regaining a semblance of her composure to say.

'It's Ellie.'

The Nightmare

I think I must have been on my way to lunch. It was difficult to be sure. The morning had been very tiring. I was confused. I was sure I had settled down in bed for the night so it wasn't easy to tell if I was completely awake or whether I was drifting away into another world. I was somewhere between the click of a light and the start of a dream and every time I closed my eyes, I began to lose myself in that world.

Although the day was bright and sunny, there was a perception in my mind of a hazy mist somewhere in the air. Maybe it was a hazy, sunny day. In any case it was a strange day.

I was walking past concrete statues and imitation greenery. They reminded me of those that decorated the square on the ground at the foot of the office block where I worked. As I walked on, I looked around and noticed a figure had emerged from the mists. It was Leah, who was now walking with me. Leah was a work colleague. She was a very attractive, dark-haired woman, with bright, light blue eyes that were the colour of the sky on a summer's day and sparkled like a clear blue ocean. I was desperately in love with Leah. My love for her was completely hopeless as she was in a relationship. Her boyfriend, John, worked in the office block next to ours. No-one ever tells you love only really works when both of you share the same feelings. Sadly, in my experience, it is an unspoken truth that often crosses our lives as we live them.

Leah flashed me a smile. Her smile could light up the greyest day and she had an enchanting personality which drew you in when you came into contact with her. She easily became friends with anyone she met.

We greeted each other. 'Hello, Leah.'

'Hello, Mike.'

As we walked on, I turned to her and said, 'Are you heading to lunch?'

'No,' she replied, 'I've got some visits to make at the Pendle Flats so I grabbed a quick snack in the office.' Pendle Flats was a five-storey residential block ahead of us near the Town Centre. They were just a short walk on and to left of the main junction into town.

'I'm heading off to Luigi's for a sandwich and coffee.' Luigi's was a small, family run, sandwich bar that I often used for lunch. It was a busy place, but there was always a friendly atmosphere, where I would be able to sit and read my daily newspaper whilst having my lunch.

As we walked on, other people were passing by us and looking over to where we were. It felt really good walking along with someone as beautiful as Leah. It was as if the passers-by were looking over and thinking how lucky I was to be with such a fabulous looking woman. As they strolled passed us, they appeared and disappeared into the misty background.

As we walked on, we soon arrived at a road crossing. It was the junction which led into the Town Centre. To the left-hand side across a small paved area was Pendle Flats.

I turned towards Leah. 'I'll see you later then.'

She smiled back. 'Of course. I'll see you later.' She turned and headed towards the flats.

I crossed the road.

When I reached the other side, I turned around and waved over to Leah. She wasn't looking and didn't notice.

I crossed the road.

When I reached the other side, I turned around and Leah gave me a short wave and smile. I waved back.

I crossed the road.

When I reached the other side, I turned around and noticed the entrance door to the flats had opened and was closing. Leah must have just gone inside. I headed into town for lunch.

It was only a short distance to Luigi's and so a few minutes later I found myself at the counter ordering my lunch. I took a seat towards the quiet part of the bar at the back. My lunch arrived and I read my newspaper.

When I had finished my meal, I gave a wave to the staff behind the counter as I left and headed back to the office.

The town was much busier than it had been earlier. The pedestrianised high street was full of people hurrying about their business and I found myself weaving in and out of them as I made my way back towards the road I had crossed earlier at the end of the Town Centre and the main road.

Finally, I arrived at the crossing. As I walked across, I noticed a group of people had gathered on the paved area ahead. They were very agitated by something.

I walked over to them and enquired 'Is everything alright? Has something happened?' A number of them pointed up towards Pendle Flats.

I looked over to the flats and saw a rough looking man framed in one of the third-floor windows. He was shouting angrily although I couldn't make out exactly what he was saying.

Looking closer, I noticed that he had someone held in a headlock. A woman. To my horror I realised that it was Leah! I think I felt my legs buckle slightly in shock as I took in the full gravity of the situation. I could hear her weakly calling for help.

I turned back to the crowd. 'We must do something,' I said anxiously. As I faced them, they started to drift away and as they thinned out, I made after one or two of them.

'Don't go. We need to help her. Please. You must help!'

It was all to no avail. They continued to walk away, fading into the mist, until I was standing in the square alone. I turned back to the flats the man was waving his fist with one hand whilst he held Leah with the other.

I had to do something. Decision made. I headed towards Pendle Flats. As I approached the door I looked towards the flat where the man was with Leah. He wasn't there. I turned around to see if anyone had decided to follow along and help me but there was no-one. I opened the entrance door into the block, walked in and proceeded up the stairs.

As I made my way up the stairs, I was thinking about what I would do when I reached the flat. My mind was racing and confused. By the time I reached the floor where the flat was, I still didn't have any real plan formulated. I knew I had to get Leah out of there and that was the extent of my mission. I was nervous and my heart was pounding as I continued on through into the corridor. The corridor had six flats along it, three on the left, three on the right. Immediately ahead of me on the left was a small alcove which led into a lift lobby. I walked slowly and quietly down the corridor trying to calm myself down as I took each step closer to the impending confrontation. Finally, I reached the flat at the end on the left-hand side. I turned to face the large, grey door, took a deep breath and knocked.

No answer.

I knocked a second time.

Still nothing.

I went to knock a third time when suddenly the door cracked open. It opened further to reveal the man at the window. He was a little taller and much stockier than me. His dark, wavy somewhat dishevelled, hair matched by a dark, scruffy beard. He looked like the archetypal villain you see in cinema cartoons.

'What do you want?' he said gruffly, his eyes staring manically back at me.

I couldn't see Leah in the flat but nevertheless I responded. 'I've come for Leah.' As soon as I said it, it seemed an inadequate response but the best I could muster in that moment.

'Go away.' He slammed the door shut in my face.

I stood stunned. I knew I couldn't just leave it there. I needed to try again.

I knocked again. This time the door opened immediately. He looked more agitated and Leah was standing at the far wall looking very frail and tearful.

'Are you deaf? I said go away,' he shouted.

'Not without Leah. I'm not going without—'

He interrupted me 'I've told you to go away. So, go!'

He slammed the door again.

I was taken aback initially but regained my resolve. I needed to get some help. I really wasn't going to sort this out on my own. I decided to head back to the lift lobby.

I pushed the button to call the lift. The lift arrived and stopped. The door opened to reveal the same man looking angrier. Leah was sitting on the floor, sobbing.

'I've come to get Leah.'

He pushed me back from the door and shouted, 'I've already told you once. Now piss off!' The door slammed shut.

I turned to the right. There was a door ahead of me. I walked quickly towards it and through into the square in front of the flats.

There were a number of people milling around busily going about their business. I wandered passed a few of them. Then in the distance, approaching me from the town, I noticed Leah's manager. As she got closer, I went over to her.

'Anne, you've got to come along quickly. Leah's been taken hostage by a mad man.' She glanced briefly towards me but continued walking on. 'Anne, please you must help her. We need to get her some help.'

Anne walked past. There were other managers also walking by. Eventually, Anne turned to me and looked down at a pocket watch she had in her hand. 'I've got a meeting. I can't stop. I might be late.'

'But you don't understand. It's Leah. She's in serious trouble.' Anne walked on. 'Why won't you help?' I pleaded despairingly but to no avail.

Anne shrugged her shoulders and walked on.

I considered approaching the other Managers but they were all bustling passed me at speed as if I wasn't there and they proceeded on their way undisturbed. I was disgusted with them. I stood for a short while distressed and angry at their ambivalence.

Eventually, I turned back towards the flats. I stared over at the building trying to work out what I could do next. I knew I still hadn't any real plan but I needed to do something.

I headed back into the building and started back up the stairs.

After a couple of flights, I bumped into another man. He was quite stocky and wearing a grey uniform.

'Where are you going?' he asked.

'There's someone being held hostage on the third floor. She's a work colleague of mine. I've come to get her out.'

'I know. I heard her screaming. I'm the security officer here. I'm sure we can sort this out.'

'OK.'

'Follow me.'

I followed him up and through the stairwell doors

into the corridor.

I knocked on the door of the flat. The door opened it was Leah's captor again. He stared maniacally back. 'I've already told you. Leave me alone. Go away.'

He started to slam the door in my face again but the security officer stepped in.

He spoke directly to the man at the door. 'Listen carefully. We have a car downstairs. It can take you to the airport so you can make your escape.' He paused. 'But you need to come out so that we can get you away.'

The man paused as if in thought. 'I'll need a helicopter to be ready for me at the airport to take me away to a distant island where I will be safe.'

'It's all been arranged just as you wish.'

This all sounded a little odd. I wasn't aware of any of this. I wasn't sure whether he might have made this up as a ruse to get him out of the flat or whether my mind was playing tricks on me again.

He beckoned me back down the corridor to two alcoves on either side. We both hid in opposite alcoves.

After a short while the flat door opened.

'He's coming out.' He mouthed over to me. The ruse was working.

I could hear footsteps approaching down the corridor and Leah whimpering weakly.

The Security officer mouthed back over to me. 'Keep quiet. Get ready.'

As they both came alongside us, the man was holding Leah tightly by her arm. We pounced, tackling both of them and he released his grip on Leah. There was a brief struggle but the Security officer threw the man onto the floor. He had overwhelmed him. The hostage taker was motionless as the Security officer held him down. Leah lay frozen in fear beside him.

'Get her out of here. Don't worry I'll deal with this guy,' he shouted over to me.

I stood up and offered Leah my hand. She took it and she got to her feet. 'We'd better go.' I gestured towards the stairwell door. We made our way towards the stairs and then started down them.

'Are you OK?'

Leah still looked shaken. She whispered quietly, 'Yes, I think so.'

I placed a comforting arm around her shoulder. 'Let's get you out of here.'

A few steps later and we were outside. It was now twilight. The sun had just set and a big crowd had gathered. Leah started to tidy herself up.

Shortly afterwards the Security officer appeared at the entrance doorway with the man we had tackled. He bundled him into a nearby police car that had turned up.

I turned back to Leah. She had spotted someone at the far side of the crowd. It was her boyfriend, John.

She went running over to him and fell into his arms.

After what seemed to be a brief conversation between them, they disappeared up the street.

The nightmare was over.

These events all happened a couple of years ago.

Shortly afterwards we both moved on to different jobs, in different places.

I was taken aback when I saw Leah today. She was walking down the other side of the street looking as beautiful and radiant as ever.

She didn't notice me.

Nemesis

1

The bar was busy. Naomi sat in a quiet room tucked away at the corner of the Pub. She had chosen this meeting place purposefully. It was quiet and there was a door beside the alcove where she was sitting. A small round table in front of her was empty. She held a shoulder bag tight against her right-hand side.

Nobody in the main bar had noticed her quietly entering through the door earlier. It was too noisy. They were all distracted by the TV screen which was in evidence high on a wall on the far side. The sporting event being shown on the screen was keeping them captivated as it played out before them.

She was wearing a full length dark-coloured coat, concealing the brighter clothing she wore underneath it. That clothing was more noticeable. She didn't want to be noticed at this particular moment.

She glanced up at a clock to check the time. The Minister she was waiting for was due at any moment. She prepared herself and waited.

It was not long to wait. No more than two or three minutes later she heard footsteps coming through the door and a man walked in. He was a stockily built man dressed smartly in a suit and tie. It was the Minister. He immediately spotted her sitting calmly in the alcove. He looked around nervously.

'Are you my escort?' he whispered.

She nodded.

He still seemed unsure of himself. 'What is your name?' Naomi didn't answer so he followed his question up quickly. 'Er, would you like a drink?' He turned around and looked up towards the empty bar counter in the room.

As he turned back towards her, Naomi had already stood up and was holding a gun in her right hand. It was aimed at him. She fired once. It hit the mark. Straight between the eyes.

The Minister's body jolted back as the bullet hit. His right foot stepped back a little before his body dropped lifeless to the floor.

Naomi had already left and was making her way down the street before turning into a quiet side road and striding along focussed on the way ahead. She reached a busy street and continued between the crowds making their way along it. She headed for the underground station a short distance away. Reaching its stairwell, she stepped down into the entrance and was swallowed by the night.

Back in the Pub, the noise in the main bar had distracted

everyone from what had happened in the side room. It was almost ten minutes before a barmaid noticed the Minister's murdered body lying lifeless on the floor. She screamed.

A number of the customers came over. They looked on horrified at the scene. One of them, an older man, emerged from the crowd and kneeled down to check for signs of life.

'He's dead.'

The manager pushed his way through whilst another work colleague comforted the barmaid.

He checked the body. 'He is dead.' He looked up to the round table where Naomi had been sitting earlier. There was no sign that anyone else had been there except for what looked like a business card on the table.

He picked it up and read it. It read 'My name is Nemesis'.

2

As he peered out of the window, he could see the beautiful landscape laid out before him as the sun rose higher in the sky and lit up the bright new day. In the distance, on a clear day, it was possible to make out the buildings of the city many miles away on the horizon. Today it was a little hazy in the distance but occasionally one could make out the shapes of recognisable buildings. He stared out of the window towards them momentarily lost in thought.

The newspapers had arrived.

He moved over towards the table where they lay and sat down. Slowly he began to thumb through each one of them carefully.

One story dominated. All the front pages had differing versions of the same event. A government minister had been shot dead in a bar close to Parliament. The details were sketchy but whoever had carried this out had not been seen. Some of the editors were suggesting that it was the work of a member of an organisation of anarchists that was terrorising the political and business community. It was all guesswork. They had a name, but it too was shrouded in mystery.

As he read on, he stroked his chin thoughtfully. He was more aware of the organisation they were talking about than anyone could have imagined. The actual incident, though, was something he knew nothing about.

He made a swift decision and immediately picked up his phone and made a call.

A woman answered. 'Hello.'

'It's Orcus.'

'Yes.'

'Get me Nemesis.'

'Understood.'

They both hung up.

3

The Royal Hotel had had a busy day hosting a conference of national representatives from the world of business and politics. After many hours of presentations and discussions, their meeting had now adjourned and they had all reconvened in a nearby suite for dinner.

The hotel staff, who had been buzzing around servicing the meeting, were now able to relax a little whilst kitchen, catering, waiters and other colleagues took over. They were all pulling together to ensure the evening meal went smoothly and everybody was satisfied with their experience.

Meanwhile, Ben was sitting in a comfortable chair close to the entrance to the suite. He was aware that the dinner was under way in the room behind him. The hotel reception was situated to his left between him and the main entrance. It was also busy dealing with incoming guests and their visitors.

He checked his watch, then rose from his seat and made his way as inconspicuously as possible through the busy reception area glancing back briefly to where he had been sitting.

When he reached the main entrance, he turned left

onto the pavement and as luck would have it, a bus pulled up just ahead of him. He boarded it. His journey took him down the street and past a couple of junctions before the bus took a right-hand turn down a quieter street.

Ben stepped off of the bus and walked into a nearby shopping mall. As he did so he heard a distant noise. He checked his watch again. It was probably the sound of his bomb detonating back at the hotel. He crossed through the mall and exited at the other side. He could hear the first sirens from the emergency services echoing around the distant streets. He looked up and then spotting a black car parked ahead of him, opened the back door and jumped in. There were two people in the front seats, a man and a woman. They both turned around in unison.

Ben gave a thumbs up. 'Job done,' he said calmly and authoritatively.

They both nodded and smiled, then putting the car into gear, drove away.

4

Naomi was sitting quietly at a table in a city coffee bar. It was busy. There was a small espresso in front of her on the table. She had chosen to sit there because it had four spaces, including her own, by the table. This was good. She was expecting company. As usual, Naomi had chosen a convenient seat, she was cautious, she didn't anticipate any trouble, but she knew if there were any problems, she would be more than ready to deal with them.

Moments later the door to the coffee bar opened and Ben and Fennelly walked in. She recognised them immediately. She knew she could handle them.

They walked up to her table and the three of them greeted each other.

Ben spoke first. 'Hi. My codename is Typhon. My colleague here is known as Leuce.'

Naomi scowled slightly at them both, then beckoned them to sit down.

Ben continued. 'We know you are operating as Nemesis,' he said quietly checking around the coffee bar that no one was in earshot. Naomi stared blankly back at him. 'We are interested in the outcomes that you are trying to achieve. Things that we are both pursuing—'

'Like what?'

'Vengeance. Retribution.'

Naomi didn't respond.

Fennelly began to speak. 'We believe we can pool our resources in a way which may prove to be beneficial to us all.'

'All?' Naomi enquired.

'We are seeking the same ends. We want change too. We want a new society. A better society.'

'You mean your society,' Naomi said, somewhat dismissively.

'Well, yes. But a society that we can all believe in.'

'Ah. There's that word 'all' again.'

Fennelly looked a little annoyed by Naomi's tone. Ben took up the conversation.

'We have a target. A big figure. Someone we believe you would be able to help us with.' Once again Naomi didn't respond but alternated her gaze from Ben to Fennelly and then back. 'Our organisation is aware of what you have done. We think if you were to join us, we can eliminate this target together. Then we can achieve our goals.'

Naomi made another dismissive gesture with her hand and turned her head away from them.

She turned back and said scornfully, 'you say you know of me. You know nothing.'

Another silence.

'We need your expertise,' Fennelly responded eventually.

Another silence.

Naomi broke the silence this time. 'So, who is it? Who is this target of yours?'

Ben and Fennelly looked at each other for confirmation. Fennelly nodded to Ben.

'OK,' Ben said.

Fennelly reached into her small handbag. Naomi stiffened and moved toward her own. Then Fennelly produced a photo which she passed to Naomi under the side of the table. Naomi stared at the picture. She betrayed no emotion on her face as she returned the photo to Fennelly.

She returned her gaze to Ben and Fennelly. She was deep in thought. Eventually she spoke slowly and calmly. 'OK Leuce, Typhon or whatever you want to call yourselves.' Her words were characteristically blunt. 'I've seen your photo. As it happens, it is someone that I had been looking at too. But listen to this and listen carefully. You don't know me. You think you know me. You know nothing about me. Your goals are not my goals. I am not interested in any of your political nonsense. I have my own motivation and it's very different from yours. But this target of yours ...' her voice trailed off. She stared thoughtfully at Ben and

Fennelly. 'I'll do this thing but on my own terms. I'm not joining your group.' She stared contemptuously at them each in turn. 'But I will do this. Are you willing to do a deal? To do my deal?'

Ben looked at her a little stunned and in a tetchy voice said, 'What. You think that—' He was stopped by Fennelly's hand.

'OK,' Fennelly said calmly. 'We'll accept "your terms" as you put it, but we'll need you to prove that you can be trusted. If not ...'

'You can trust me.'

'Good.'

They all shook hands. Ben and Fennelly got up from their seats. 'We'll be in touch,' Fennelly said very deliberately. They left the coffee bar.

Outside as they walked away, Ben looked quizzically at Fennelly.

'What just happened?'

Fennelly looked sterner now. 'We need her. Orcus wants her. We can use her, but I don't trust her.'

5

The financial district of the city was centred around a main junction. It had six roads feeding into it and a subway enabling pedestrians to cross between the roads safely. At one end of the junction was the target. A large financial institution set atop a series of steps which terraced down to the subway entrance on the street below. The area was becoming crowded. It was close to lunchtime and people were funnelling out of the building and down the steps in increasing numbers.

Perses, his codename, stood by the subway entrance. He looked elderly with a distinct stoop and held what appeared to be a walking stick.

At another end of the junction, Ben looked on, intermittently checking the time. He made sure he had visual contact with Perses from across the street. A woman emerged from behind the wall Ben was standing against. It was Fennelly. He held up his wrist towards her and pointed at his watch. They both nodded. He checked the time once more and then gave the pre-arranged signal to Perses as he waited across the junction.

Perses took his stick and began prodding at

something on the kerb close to where he was standing. The stick found its target. A series of fuses hidden by the kerb which would activate nearby firecrackers. With the fuses activated, Perses disappeared into the subway.

Seconds later the firecrackers began to go off. As planned, the sound they made replicated the sound of gunshots. Many people exiting the building froze in fear or ran back to take cover inside the building.

Ben and Fennelly had already walked away from the junction and down the street away from the building and towards a nearby river crossing.

Ben checked the time again. He held his hand up in front of Fennelly and mouthed 'Five seconds.' Five seconds later a loud explosion boomed from the building. Smoke billowed out from the front entrance. There was the sound of screaming. Now people were emerging from the smoke-filled building in panic, some were coughing, some appeared to be injured and others were carrying colleagues unsteadily towards the steps. It was chaos.

Ben and Fennelly walked on, a little faster than before.

Perses emerged from a subway exit at the far side of the junction from where he had been a few moments earlier. He looked completely different. He had discarded his walking stick; his stoop had gone and he now looked like a much younger and fitter man. He turned briefly to check out the destruction behind him. Then he quickly headed away, down another street, which led to a bridge which would take him across the river and on to the far bank.

6

The room was crowded with people. Around a couple of dozen, Naomi thought. She was sat impassively at the back in the corner whilst Fennelly stood at the front briefing everyone for the evening's operation.

Naomi had already taken in her instructions and was finding the whole situation in the room a little unnerving. They were all zealots, fanatics seeking to further their cause. She was merely settling a grievance and the chance to do it on a target she could otherwise have found difficult to get access to on her own. This was her motivation to put up with all the nonsense going on around her. She fiddled around in her bag checking she had everything ready. She was steely in her determination and ready to deal with any problems that she may or may not encounter in the next few hours.

Still Fennelly continued on. They were dividing into smaller groups, assessing the location, places to find cover and methods of escape. Finally, she finished. She checked the timings with everyone and addressed the room one final time.

'OK. To your positions. Good luck. Stay focussed and we will all be back to toast our success. To success.'

7

As the Prime Minister stepped out of the car and the cavalcade drew to a halt, a woman's arm appeared between two figures who were part of the crowd that had gathered alongside. It was Naomi. A split second later a shot rang out and she withdrew her arm. The shot had hit its target. Straight between the eyes.

She had already begun walking away when the armed security guards leapt out of their cars and sprang into action. Ben and Fennelly's teams were waiting for them in their pre-assigned positions. An exchange of gunshots started.

Ben fired then weaved away and over a nearby low wall for cover, joining two other members of his team who were also firing towards the guards. They were able to pick off a number of guards from the relative safety of their position hidden by the wall and the dimly lit evening shadows.

Fennelly's group were on the other side and she sped towards them at a pace pausing only briefly as she caught sight of Naomi disappearing into the distance. The hesitation was enough for her to take a bullet in the leg. Her leg buckled as she dropped down on her wounded knee. Quickly, she rose to her feet but to no avail as a volley of bullets peppered her body. Weakly, she whispered 'Nemesis' as she slumped to the ground. Lifeless.

Naomi meanwhile had walked out and away from all the commotion. She had already planned her route. She turned to walk down a nearby footpath leaving the gun fire behind her. Her determined manner went unnoticed by the others as she left them behind and, as usual, her focus was on her exit from the fray. The footpath was no more than a wide alleyway bordered by a wall on one side and fencing on the other. It was a walk of around fifty yards to a street where she would complete her getaway. As she walked on, the firestorm behind her was beginning to quieten. She looked up and along towards the end of the alleyway. A black car had pulled up. It looked like the getaway car that had been arranged for her. Then she noticed a figure emerge at the end of the alley, silhouetted by the street light beyond. The figure stood at the end where the footpath met the street. His demeanour made Naomi uneasy.

She didn't have much time to react. A split second later a shot rang out and a body hit the ground.

Maybe five or ten seconds later the car pulled away into the night.

Silence.

Just a few short moments later, armed figures emerged at the other end of the street. Guns drawn; they ran towards the area where the alley ended. They stopped as they spotted the body on the ground. One of them noticed something on the ground nearby. It looked like a card of some description. He bent down to pick it up. His gaze remained on the body until eventually, as his other colleagues arrived around him, he turned his attention to the card. He turned it over and swore loudly. The card read 'My Name is Nemesis.'

When Love Dies

1

Luciana held up the navy-blue jacket and waved it accusingly at her boyfriend who was standing across the room from her.

'I can smell your tart on this!' she said contemptuously. 'It smells of her cheap perfume.'

Her boyfriend, Dave, waved her comments away dismissively and turned to walk away.

She strode over towards him, still brandishing the offending jacket. 'Don't you just walk away from me. I can smell her on it. It's disgusting.' She pushed the jacket into his face as he turned back.

'You're talking shit!' he yelled angrily at her and struck her across the face with the back of his hand.

She reeled back in pain. He stepped towards her and hit her again. This time she crumbled to the floor, dropping the jacket as she fell. She clutched her face as the pain from his blows overpowered the emotional pain she had originally felt on the discovery of the jacket.

He stomped off towards the door and as he reached it, stopped and turned back to her. 'You're the whore. I wish you were dead. You're an ugly cow. Why don't you just piss off.'

He slammed the door behind him and left the house.

Luciana picked the jacket up off of the floor from where it had landed and threw it angrily at the door. Then she slumped to the floor onto her knees and began to cry.

The days and weeks that followed saw Luciana and Dave's relationship fracturing even further. Dave had become more controlling and spent most of his time either with his friends or in his shed in the garden. Luciana was often confined to the house and Dave was becoming more and more suspicious of her friends and their influence on her.

One particular night they had had another row.

'I'm going out,' Dave said.

'Where?'

'It's none of your business.'

'Are you meeting your tart again?' Luciana said in a manner that made her feelings all too obvious.

'I've told you. It's none of your business.' He paused then continued. 'Actually, I'm meeting up with some mates.'

Luciana swaggered up to him. 'That's OK. I'm going out with my mates too.'

He looked back at her. A serious look. 'No, you're not.'

'I am,' she insisted.

He shook his head and disappeared to get ready to go

out, leaving Luciana standing, hands belligerently on her hips. After a few moments she returned to the front room.

Hearing the front door close, she peered out to see Dave leaving as he had said earlier.

Ten to fifteen minutes later she readied herself to leave. She walked to the front door and, trying the handle, realised it had been locked. She delved into her handbag to look for her keys. They were missing. He'd locked her in.

Luciana stood in disbelieve for a few moments, then the feeling of anger replaced her incredulity. She spun around and headed for the exit by the back door. That was locked too. The key was missing.

Increasingly exasperated, she stormed over to a drawer where they kept the spare keys. They'd also disappeared. She rummaged through the drawer frantically becoming angrier and more desperate.

She was completely locked in with no obvious way out.

Pulling the drawer fully out, she threw it at a nearby wall. Parts of it smashed and its contents were strewn around the floor. She thought to herself, *I'll trash his precious garden shed.* Then realised she couldn't get out into the garden. Foolish. More annoyed. Instead, she continued smashing items around the room indiscriminately and often without any real reasoning.

Some of them were items she liked. It didn't matter anymore.

Once her rampage was over, she cried. Then went to bed still raging and still hitting out at anything within range.

In the days that followed, their rowing became more bitter and happened more often.

He shouted at her, 'I know you've been seeing other men!'

'I haven't,' she protested.

'Have you slept with them?'

She would shout, 'you've been shagging her again, haven't you?' when he didn't arrive home at night.

He told her. 'I still love you, Lu.'

'You love hitting me.'

'I love you.'

Luciana would bare her body. 'I have bruises that say otherwise.'

2

Elena was draped across her armchair staring at the screen on her phone and flicking through the pages of the app she had opened. She checked the time. It was late in the evening. Leaning forward she took a sip from the glass of pinot on the table nearby.

The doorbell rang.

She looked quizzically towards the door. It was as if she was questioning why it had rung at this time of the night. Getting up out of the armchair she walked over to the front window and peered out into the darkness.

A bedraggled figure was standing on the footpath by the porch. It was a woman. Elena thought she recognised her and walked over to the hallway and opened the door.

Luciana looked up as if she was about to speak.

'Lucy. What's happened?' Elena was immediately concerned about the demeanour of her friend.

'I need somewhere to stay,' Luciana said flatly in a very downbeat voice.

'Come in, Lucy.' Elena ushered Luciana into the hallway. Luciana was carrying a trolley case and a hand-held suitcase.

She shook her head sorrowfully. 'Oh Elena. What

have I done?'

'What's up? What's happened?'

Luciana put her case down and looked up.

'I've left him, Elena. For good. I can't go back. Not anymore.' She paused and bowed her head again. 'Not ever.'

Elena helped Luciana remove her coat. Then gave her a hug.

Luciana pulled back a little. 'Can I stay for a while? Just until I straighten myself out.'

Elena smiled and hugged her again. 'Of course you can, Lucy. Of course you can.'

The following morning Luciana woke up on Elena's sofa. She was disorientated at first by the strange surroundings but as the full extent of the events of the previous night came back to her, she began to come to terms with where she was.

Elena was in the kitchen. Hearing her friend moving around, she peered round into the room. 'Fancy a cup of tea?'

Luciana nodded.

'How are you feeling this morning?'

'I'm fine.' She paused remembering all of the things that had happened yesterday. Elena brought her the tea. 'I can't go back, Elena. Not now. He's been hitting me again.' She felt a bruise on her arm. 'It's too dangerous. He's too dangerous.'

'You'll be OK here, Lucy.'

'You must understand if I'd stayed any longer, I would have killed him. Or he would have killed me.'

Elena stroked her friend's back comfortingly and smiled. 'It's OK.'

'I promise I won't be a burden. I won't stay long.' She paused and began staring out of a nearby window and into the distance. 'I do wish I was back home though. Back in Italy I mean. I came here to start a new life. A bright new future. Look at me now!' She was touching her face gingerly. Was there another bruise on the side of her face too? 'I should never have come here. I was happy in Florence. I wanted adventure. I think I've got more than I bargained for.'

Elena continued to comfort her. 'It's OK, Lucy. Stay here a while. Straighten things out and when you're ready to move on ... I'm sure things will work out.'

3

Elena was walking down the street on her way to work when she bumped into Gulya. Gulya was a friend and like Elena, from an eastern European background, but unlike Elena she was from Russia. She was with her youngest child tucked comfortably into a pushchair.

They greeted one another. 'Hi Gulya.'

'Hi.'

Elena looked down at the youngster. 'How's the little one?'

'Oh, he's fine. How's Luciana? I heard that she was staying with you.'

'She's OK. Perhaps a little lost at the moment though. I guess she's got a lot of decisions to make since she walked out on Dave.'

'Really!' Gulya seemed startled by Elena's comments. Dave and Luciana were also friends with Gulya and her husband, Max. She continued, 'Max told me Dave had thrown her out.'

'Oh. That's interesting,' Elena said thoughtfully. 'Lucy does seem a bit confused sometimes. She also told me he was going to move his girlfriend in with him.'

'It does sound muddled as you say.'

'I'm not even sure whether Dave is legally allowed to kick her out. I mean, I know they're not actually married but even so.'

Gulya nodded. 'I don't suppose we'll really know what happened. I remember Max also said Dave hoped she'd come back.'

Elena shook her head. 'I don't think that's likely. I'm pretty sure he treated her quite badly.'

'Did he?'

'So, I understand. She does seem to be quite broken by it all.'

'So, how long do you expect she will stay at your place?'

Elena shrugged. 'I'm not sure. Just until she sorted things out, I suppose. Then she'll move on. It is nice to have the company though.'

When Elena arrived home later that day, she found Luciana had left a note for her. It read *"I've gone out. I'm going to make him pay for all this. Luciana"*

Elena scratched her head. She was bewildered. The note was a little mysterious in that there seemed to be no particular reason that could have provoked her friend's reaction. Other than what had happened in the past of course. She sat down in a chair trying to rationalise what she had read and understand what might have happened since they had last spoken.

She picked up her phone and called Luciana. It rang

a couple of times and then went to voicemail. Elena rang another couple of times leaving what she felt was a slightly garbled message.

'Lucy. Please call me back. Please, Lucy. Let's talk. I'm sure we can sort this out. Please call me.'

She never returned the call.

When Luciana finally arrived back it was late. Elena noticed a strange smell on her clothes. She struggled to recognise it. They both settled down for the night without much being said. Only after getting into bed did Elena think that she had identified the aroma from earlier. It reminded her of painting or decorating she thought. Perhaps something like turpentine. She struggled to get to sleep for some time worrying about what her friend had done.

In the morning, she decided to speak to Luciana during their breakfast.

'What exactly did you do, Lucy?' she asked.

'I've trashed his new car,' came the reply.

4

Elena was in the kitchen with Luciana getting a meal together when they were interrupted by a loud banging at the door.

Elena walked around to the window to see the source of the banging. She turned in horror to Luciana and whispered 'It's Dave!'

Luciana looked horrified. 'What do I do?'

'Stay in the kitchen, Lucy. Let me deal with him.'

Another series of heavy blows boomed out from the door. A man's voice shouted 'Come out here you bitch. I know you're in there.'

Elena stood at the other side of the closed door as it shook under the barrage.

'Who is it?'

'It's Dave. Get that bloody cow out here.'

'Lucy's not here, Dave.'

'You cow. You've ruined my new car,' Dave shouted loudly from the porch.

'Lucy's not here.'

'I don't believe you. I want to see her now.'

'But she's gone out. She's not here.'

'That evil cow has destroyed my car. I want to see

her here right now.'

'I'm not opening the door, Dave. She's not here. Please calm down.'

He continued pounding on the door. 'Open up this door or I'll break the bloody thing down.'

'Calm down, Dave.' He continued the banging, shaking the door as he did so. 'Please, please go away. Lucy's not here. If you don't go away, I'll have to call the police.'

'She's in there. I know she is!' He thumped on the door even louder.

'Dave, you must believe me she's not here. She's gone out. You're scaring me. Please go away. I'm here on my own.'

'I'm going nowhere until she comes out here. She's wrecked my car. I'm going to sue the cow for every last penny she owns.'

He pounded on the door some more. Then as quickly as it had begun it stopped. Elena stood shaking in the hallway and then crept over to the window to see what had happened. She spotted Luciana peering around from the kitchen door. Looking outside, she saw Dave had walked back down to the path along to the roadway. A police car pulled up.

She whispered over to Luciana. 'It's the police.'

Luciana looked startled. 'I didn't call them.'

Elena shrugged. 'Me neither. It must have been one

of the neighbours.'

'He'll blame me.'

Elena shrugged again then turned back to watch the conversation he was having with the police. It continued for some minutes before Dave slowly started to walk away. She watched as he wandered back down the road, stopping occasionally to shout back towards the police. They waved him away. Once he had gone and everything had calmed down a police officer walked up to Elena's door. He knocked.

Elena opened it gingerly. She had the security chain on.

'Afternoon Ma'am. Are you alright in here?'

Elena nodded. 'Yes. A bit shaken but I'm OK.'

'It should be fine now, Ma'am. The gentleman has gone home. You shouldn't be concerned anymore.'

'Thanks officer.'

'How do you know him?'

'He's a friend's ex. I think he thought she was here.'

'Oh, I see. Well, as I say, everything should be OK now.'

'Thanks again.'

The officer turned and walked away. Elena shut the door and returned to the window. The police car stayed around for a short while before finally moving off. Everything was quiet again. Luciana emerged from the kitchen.

'All clear?' she asked. Elena nodded.

Elena shook her head despairingly. 'What on earth have you done to his car? What happened yesterday?'

'I just bought some paint and white spirit.'

'Why?'

'Let's just say I've sort of redecorated it.'

Elena looked shocked. 'Oh my God. What have you done?'

Luciana looked over and smiled a little. 'I guess made it look more decorative. That's all.'

5

A few days later Elena was relaxing in her garden when Luciana appeared at the front gate. She stumbled down the footpath bleeding, dishevelled and holding her left arm. She looked distressed and in pain.

'Lucy!' Elena called out, 'what on earth has happened?' She rushed over to her friend and cradled her weak body in her arms. Luciana's face was wet with tears.

'He cornered me down the street,' she said slowly and quietly as if each word was stabbing at her as she spoke it.

'Dave?'

Luciana nodded.

'Oh Lucy. Let's get you inside and clean you up.' She gently supported Luciana as they made their way slowly indoors. Elena led her to the kitchen sink and then proceeded to clean up the wounds and bruises. Luciana winced with each dab on her skin. Elena worked her way around the visible marks, finishing up back at the cut on her face. 'It doesn't look too bad now, Lucy. Not great but OK.'

Luciana looked up. 'My arm is really painful. I might

have broken something.'

'Can you lift it up?'

Luciana shook her head. 'I don't think so.' She winced in pain as she tried unsuccessfully.

Elena looked at her thoughtfully. 'I think we'd better get you to A&E. Let them check you out properly.'

Luciana started crying again as Elena took her back in her arms. 'I want to go home,' she wailed. 'Why did I ever leave Italy? I'm such a mess.' The tears flowed even more.

'Come on Lucy. It'll be alright. We'll get you checked out first. They'll know best.' She smiled reassuringly at Luciana.

Lifting up her head to face Elena, Luciana nodded weakly through her tear-stained cheeks and they made their way out and to the hospital.

They were gone for many hours and by the time they returned to Elena's house the rest of the day was over and it was the early hours of the morning. Luciana's arm wasn't broken, but the hospital had patched her up and given her some painkillers to help her sleep. They both settled down for the night.

The next day Elena was up first and brought her friend a hot drink as she lay on the sofa.

'How did you sleep?'

'Not very well.'

'Was it the pain?' she enquired.

'Too much on my mind. The pain as well. I think the tablets helped a little bit.'

Elena stroked her friend's good arm softly and tenderly. Luciana forced a smile and sipped her drink.

'Thanks.'

'It's OK, Lucy.'

'No, I mean thanks for everything.'

'I still think we should have contacted the police.'

Luciana didn't respond but continued to sip her drink quietly.

'He might come back again,' Elena persisted.

Luciana stared blankly into space and after a long pause spoke. 'No. I think that'll make things worse. I need to deal with it so he won't bother me again.'

Elena looked back at her slightly puzzled and worried by what her words might mean. 'Don't do anything silly though, will you?'

6

Some days later, Elena was arriving back home late in the day when as she arrived Luciana came hurtling out of the front door. Her face was contorted in a rage.

'Lucy what's up? What's happened?' Elena said, trying to grab her friend as she flew past her.

'He's done it now. He's really done it now.'

'What Lucy? Dave? What's he done?'

Luciana paused briefly. 'He's only gone and moved that tart in with him.' She began to move away again.

'But Lucy...' Elena lost her loose grip on Luciana as her words trailed off. She called after her, 'you told me that before. You knew about that already.'

'He'd threatened to but now he's actually gone and done it,' Luciana shouted back as she stormed away down the footpath. 'The bastard's going to pay for this.' Her voiced trailed off as she went passed the gate. Slamming it shut in her rage.

'Lucy. No.' Elena called after her. 'Don't. Don't be silly. Don't do anything silly.'

It was too late. Luciana was already disappearing down the street and into the distance and out of earshot. Elena began to walk after her but Luciana was outpacing her and too far away. She stopped after just a few steps and, realising the futility of her pursuit, turned and walked slowly and pensively back to the house.

Once inside and into the front room she found an empty bottle of wine on the floor and a glass, also drained of its contents, nearby. The conclusion was clear. Luciana had been drinking and finished off that bottle and another one she subsequently found in the kitchen. Elena feared the worst.

The walk to Dave's house only took Luciana a little more than ten minutes. When she arrived there, she noticed that there was a light on in the front of the house. She crept up closer to the window. The curtains were drawn but still she tried to peer inside to see who she might be able to see. But to no avail; she saw nothing.

Although she was still in a fury, her demeanour had changed and she tiptoed quietly around the outside of the house. As she did so, it occurred to her that she could slip silently around the side and into the back garden.

The garden was very dark and, in the dim lights from the house, finding her footing was proving a challenge. She could make out the outline of Dave's precious garden shed. The door had been pushed to but opened with a minimum of force. She felt her way around inside, trying to remember where various tools and equipment would be placed.

A noise from the house startled her and, for a second, she froze on the spot. She turned and listened carefully. Dave seemed to be heading out into the garden. Stealthily, but with her heart racing, she felt her way around to the outside of the shed and to the back where she could find some cover.

Then she peered around the corner and could see Dave's silhouette as he arrived at the shed door and began to look around. He took a couple of steps towards the place where she was hiding. She backed off and tiptoed slowly to the other side. Eventually she emerged at the front again but to her horror Dave was still there.

She paused to gather her thoughts.

He had his back to her at the far side of the shed door. She tried to remain silent but was concerned he might sense she was there.

He began to turn towards her. She panicked and grabbed a large, heavy tool from a box just inside the door. It was a molegrip. As she did so, she swung her arm in an uppercut action towards his head. He hadn't turned around and so she caught him flush on the back of his head. As she swung back down, she struck him again, this time on the top of his skull. His body contorted as he collapsed to the ground. She looked on in terror. Before he could react, she had hit him again and again. Her attack on him continued in a frenzy where he lay. She stopped hitting him and stood for a moment. Her mind was racing and her feelings muddled.

She plucked up a little courage and bent down to check his body. He was dead. She felt his blood still warm on his face. It shocked her. She stumbled as she stood back up.

She turned and ran, dropping the molegrip as she fled in to the street. Then, slowly, to a walk. As casual as she could, given the enormity of what she had just done. She headed back to Elena's in a state of both disbelief and macabre euphoria.

When she woke up the following morning, Luciana's thoughts turned to her home back in Italy. It seemed that every night her dream was the same. Being back home. Feeling the warm Tuscan sun beating down on her body. Her mother. Her father. Being young again. Carefree. Playing games in the narrow streets of Florence. Skipping playfully across the piazzas.

Happy.

She rolled over on the sofa and could see out of the window to the street beyond. A police car had pulled up outside and two officers were heading towards the house.

It was then the truth hit her and she began to cry. Her dream was over. She would never see Italy again.

The Darkest Star

1

Jenny was feeling surprisingly positive after her boyfriend, Peter, had proposed to her last night. He had always been good for her despite the continuing health issues that she had. She, of course, accepted his proposal and now they were engaged.

Although she didn't feel she was really understood by most people, even her friends and family, Peter was there for her. She wanted other people to see her as normal but that would always be an impossible thing to expect from them.

She thought about this feeling she had had for many years. It was a feeling influenced by the way that other people behaved towards her. They made it difficult for her; she often felt uncomfortable, and because of this she felt they saw her as an oddity. This left her sometimes struggling to live life the way that they could. At times she felt picked on. Or perhaps ignored. But mostly just different.

Yet, she felt she was a normal person. But she wondered whether there was anything so strange as a normal person? It was an unanswerable question.

She sat in the front room staring blankly out of the

window at the world outside. She believed she was misunderstood. She would tell her friends that she would "hold things together but often by the skin of her teeth". She laughed a little to herself. She thought she was turning "holding things together" into an art form. The positivity from last night had had a good effect on her. She put on her favourite bright orange top. She always wore this when she felt good; it would often brighten her mood even further.

Nevertheless, she still occasionally felt lost.

Jenny's train of thought was interrupted as the front gate opened. It was Peter. She waved to him as he made his way down the garden path. He waved back.

She listened as the front door opened and she turned towards the door at the other end of the lounge. Peter entered and walked over to her. They exchanged an affectionate kiss and a cuddle.

'I saw you waving at me,' Peter said as he smiled.

'I wasn't waving I was drowning,' came her reply.

His smile disappeared. 'Is everything OK?'

'Yes,' Jenny replied. 'I was just having a little joke.'

'So, you're sure you're OK then?'

Jenny took his arm. 'I'm fine. I was just deep in thought when you arrived. Nothing to worry about.'

Peter's smile returned. 'Love you, Jen.'

'I love you too, Pete.'

They kissed again. 'How are you getting used to

being an engaged lady?'

Jenny smiled too. 'It's wonderful. I'm so lucky.' They kissed again and embraced.

'Look at you, Jen,' he said, stepping back a pace. 'You're a vision in tangerine.' They both laughed and shared another kiss and embrace.

The following day Peter was getting up to go to work. Jenny was already up and having breakfast in the kitchen.

Peter entered the room and looked across to the table where she was sitting. Her food remained largely untouched. She was very quiet and looking down at the table whilst pushing her food around on the plate.

'Are you OK?' he asked softly.

She shrugged then nodded. 'I'm fine.' The response didn't satisfy his concern. She spoke quietly and without any emotion.

'Are you sure? You seem distant. Is something on your mind?'

No answer.

'If there's something troubling you perhaps it would better to talk about it. It's always good to share a problem.'

'I'm not sure if I can.'

Peter was evaluating this statement. She was clearly troubled but he knew he ought not push her if she didn't want to share whatever it was. 'Well, if you do want to talk to you know I'm here for you.' He touched her hand. She didn't respond.

Silence.

Peter was about to speak again when Jenny spoke very quietly. 'I had a dream last night.'

Peter moved closer and put his arm around her. 'Do you want to talk about it then?'

There was a further pause. Then Jenny slowly began. 'We were together in your car.' She paused to look up at Peter. 'I was driving. I was feeling really happy, like I'd never felt happier. We were going along the road for a while when I turned off into a field. We carried on across the field. Everything was normal.' She paused for a moment and looked a little worried.

'Go on. It's fine.'

'Well, next thing the field runs out and we are heading out onto the road where the cliff is. I recognised it because it was where we often go walking. Anyway, the road ended but the car continued on. I could see the cliff edge.'

Peter held her hand firmly; she was becoming more agitated, more excited.

'Suddenly, we go past the cliff and over the edge.'

'Oh Jen—'

'It was strange. I felt really good. Really positive. I felt so good and much better than I have done for a long while.' She stopped.

'Well, what happened next?'

'I don't remember. I think I woke up soon after that. I felt a little upset when I woke up that that feeling of ... well elation I suppose, had gone.'

'That is a little disturbing, Jen,' Peter said sympathetically.

'I know. But you see, afterwards I felt really positive too. After the initial shock when I woke up. After that I felt really good.'

Peter embraced her comfortingly. 'Don't worry, Jen. Everything will be alright. We'll get through this together.' He smiled. 'Remember I'm always with you. I'll never let you come to harm.'

They both hugged.

2

Jenny was making her way home. She was walking quickly and looking a little frazzled. She had put the hood on her coat up, covering her head and most of her face. This was her sign that she didn't want to talk to anyone. She wasn't feeling well. As she approached home, she noticed a couple of people standing chatting on the footpath close to her house. They looked threatening, were they watching her? Following her? She quickened her pace further as she passed them.

They were neighbours. Two elderly ladies who were just returning from the local shops.

But Jenny's mind was racing. She arrived at the gate and glanced back anxiously towards them as they continued their conversation. She met their gaze for a moment.

She began to head towards the front door. Quicker. Breathless. She was sure the ladies were moving closer to her as she reached the door.

They hadn't moved.

As she entered the house, she let out a scream, which got progressively louder as she rushed up the stairs to the safety of the bedroom. She threw her coat down, kicked off a shoe as she dived under the covers of her bed. The other shoe fell off as she landed on the bed. Silence. She began to cry.

Sometime later, Peter arrived home. He felt a little uneasy as he opened the gate and headed towards the front door. Jenny wasn't sitting in her usual seat near the window. The light was beginning to fade as dusk approached and there was no sign of any lighting in the house. Where was Jenny?

He opened the front door and walked into the darkened hallway. He peered around and called out, 'Jen.' There was no reply. He checked the front room and, as he suspected, it was empty. He turned and headed back towards the stairs. The next most obvious place she could be was the bedroom. He hadn't heard from her for a few hours, which was unusual. If she was unwell, she could be in bed.

He opened the bedroom door and immediately spotted a figure buried underneath the bed sheets. 'Jen?' Still no answer. As he approached the bed, he could see a little tress of her wavy dark brown hair poking out from under the sheets. He slowly lifted the sheet and revealed her face. It was pale, her eyes were reddened from the tears. 'Oh Jen,' he exclaimed, 'what has happened?'

She opened her eyes a little but didn't speak.

He reached over to brush the hair away from her face. She resisted at first but he managed to reveal her anxious and fearful look. 'Oh Jen. It's OK I'm here. Everything's OK.'

She looked unconvinced.

As he touched the pillow case it was damp. He assumed she had been crying for a while. 'What's happened, Jen? Can I help?'

She moved her head a little, he wasn't certain but he thought she shook it.

She looked over to him. 'They're following me, Pete,' she said, her voice weak and croaky. A pause. Then more anxiously. 'They followed me home. They're outside. They know my name. They're waiting for me.' She pulled the sheet back over her head.

'Who are, Jen?' No reply. 'I didn't see anyone outside. Perhaps they've gone.' Another silence. Peter gently lifted the bedcover up a little. Jenny had it gripped tight. He didn't force it any further.

'I saw them, Pete. I saw them,' she whispered insistently.

'It's OK Jen,' he said reassuringly.

Peter looked up across the room. The curtains were still open. 'Don't worry, Jen. I'll check out front for you.' He walked over to the window.

It was much darker now and the streetlights had come on. He peered out into the street. There were one or two people scurrying along heading home for the night. He closed the curtains.

'It's OK now, Jen. There's no-one out there anymore. Everything's fine. It's all nice and quiet. Everything's back to normal now. You're quite safe now. I'm here.'

Peter sat close to her on the side of the bed with a comforting arm on the covers across her back. He sat there for some time, pausing only to turn on the nearby bed light.

As the night moved on, he settled down alongside her for the night. Hopefully she would feel better in the morning.

The following day, Peter had been up and about for some hours when he decided it might be time to check on her. He made his way towards the stairs and immediately spotted Jenny sitting on one of the steps. She was crouched just over half way up with her head in her hands.

'Hi Jen. How are you feeling today?' he enquired. He wasn't sure if his tone was quite right. He was trying to get a balance somewhere between concerned but positive.

Jenny raised her head up. She was quite bedraggled. She said nothing.

'Would you like me to rustle up something to eat?'
She shook her head.

'What about a nice cup of tea?'

There was a long pause. Then she started to get up. Peter met her as she rose and took her hand, slowly guiding her downstairs.

Once sat at the kitchen table he began to make a drink for her.

'So, how are you today?'

Very quietly and slowly she spoke. 'I'm trying to hold things together.'

He poured out the tea for her. 'Well, just take it easy for the moment, eh?'

'I'm trying hard to, Pete. I'm not sure how successfully though.'

He sat down alongside her. 'Just take it easy, Jen. You're doing fine.'

Although Jenny's manner improved after the tea and as the day progressed, she still felt a little fragile for the next few days but, in her own way, managed to hold things together and function normally.

Despite everything, she was worried that it was still possible she could break down at a moment's notice but otherwise everything was normal now.

3

It had been a gloriously sunny day and so Jenny and Peter had decided to visit a nearby beach. After spending some time relaxing together on the sand, taking in the sun's rays and a little paddle at the water's edge they went to a nearby old fisherman's pub.

They had a few drinks, some food and a chat with some of the locals. It was a place they would often go to for a relaxing drink so they knew some of the regulars.

It had been a lovely day out.

As the sun set and night drew on, they decided to walk along to the cliffs. The place they would often visit.

It was beginning to get dark and as their time enjoying the day came to a close and the stars began to come out, they headed back towards their car.

They stopped for a while to take in the last moments. Peter was staring back along the coast as the lights came on where they had been earlier. Jenny was lost in her own thoughts, staring up at the emerging night sky.

'I like looking at the stars,' she said. 'They look so beautiful twinkling in the night sky. Don't you sometimes think they seem to watch over us as we live our lives?' She paused as Peter joined her staring into the heavens but didn't make any comment. 'They seem so far away, but over the years they are always there. The same stars. I remember them when I was young. My parents would tell me about them. Some of their names. I think one was the north star, Rigel might have been another. And many others.'

Peter studied her and her faraway gaze. She continued with her contemplation.

'I'd like to think in some way they look down on us and keep watch on us.' She went on. 'I often imagine the brightest star, that one there.' She pointed towards a particularly bright star. 'I imagine it is my grandpa and nan looking down on me. I was always really close to them. I feel they are watching over me, keeping me safe. Protecting me when I'm struggling to cope. When my demons start to overwhelm me. But when I die, I could never be one of those stars. Not any of those bright ones twinkling so beautifully. I think my spirit would be twinkling from the darkest star in the sky.'

'Oh Jen, why would you think that?'

'Because it would. It's me, my life and all the darkness that seems to overwhelm me at times.'

'Do you really feel that way?'

'Sometimes. Perhaps more often than I like to admit.'

'But you're beautiful, Jen. You shine brighter to me than anything I could ever imagine. I want so much for you, not to have these dark thoughts. We have a lifetime of joy ahead of us. We can share that joy.' He embraced her. Then after a while slowly pulled away. 'I don't see you as the darkest star, Jen. I see you as my shining light.' They kissed and embraced.

4

It had been a very busy and tiring week and by its end, Jenny and Peter were exhausted. That weekend they had planned to meet up with friends for a drink and lunch. It was the perfect way to unwind and recharge their batteries following the rigours of the recent days.

Peter drove to the pub restaurant. He could have a few drinks and then Jenny, who would drink soft drinks, juices and may be a cup of tea, could then drive back. They often did this. One would drive back so the other could drink and they would take turns in who drove back and who drank.

They arrived at the pub in the early afternoon. It was a large, restaurant bar; an old sixteenth-century building converted and updated to reflect twenty-first century fashion. It was called the Cockleboat Inn.

As Peter drove into the car park he passed their friends, Simon and Lynne, who were already walking from their car towards the entrance. As they spotted Peter's car they waved and then waited for Jenny and Peter by the entrance.

The four friends greeted each other in the doorway. Simon was an old work colleague of Peter's. They had kept in touch after Peter left some years back; now Simon had also left but both couples often enjoyed an afternoon at the Cockleboat particularly when, as it was today, the weather was fine and warm.

The Cockleboat Inn was situated close to the nearby shore and, being in a small fishing port, was unsurprisingly, noted for its seafood menu.

The bar was busy but Jenny and Lynne managed to find a nice bench table on the balcony overlooking the sea. Their partners joined them shortly after with their drinks and, after a short wait, a waitress brought their food order.

Peter and Simon would often share memories of their time working together whilst Jenny and Lynne's conversation was more about their own interests, occasionally joining in the conversation with the men after the work topic had been exhausted and the subject moved on to other things. As expected, the food was good and the drinks helped lubricate the discussion.

As the hours passed by, Peter looked over towards Jenny who was very quiet and staring out to sea. Lynne had also noticed this as Jenny's conversation had begun to dry up.

'Are you OK, Jen?' he asked. She nodded.

At the end of the afternoon the couples bid each other farewell and went their separate ways.

Peter gave Jenny the car keys and sat himself in the

passenger seat. Jenny drove off still saying nothing.

'Are you sure you're alright, Jen?' Peter said. 'You're very quiet.'

She didn't respond immediately but drove on. Peter persisted and she eventually replied.

'I'm fine. It's been a lovely day. I've never felt better.'

As they continued their journey back onto the main road home Jenny was focussed on the road ahead.

Peter was gazing idly out of the window when he realised Jenny had driven past the turning towards home. 'Jenny? That was our turning. Where are we going?'

Jenny drove on, she was staring; her eyes fixed into the distance. Suddenly, she spoke. 'You know I'm feeling really happy, like I've never felt happier.'

Peter smiled. 'I'm so pleased. I love it when you're so happy.' He went back to stare out of the window. He remembered that Jenny had said something similar about being so happy recently but was racking his brains to recall when it was.

Jenny spoke again. 'I feel so good. I think we should go for a drive to the place where we go walking by the cliffs.'

At that point, the car turned off of the road and down a footpath. Peter suddenly remembered the previous conversation he had had with Jenny and was jolted by sudden fear as the car sped up and left the road. His mind flashed back to that conversation.

Jenny smiled and in a strange voice continued. 'It's like a wonderful dream. I feel so good, so positive and much better than I have felt for a long while. Finally, the pain has gone.'

Peter was now very alarmed; he reached across the car and called out. 'Jenny what are you doing? Where are you going? Stop Jenny. No. Jenny! No. Jennifer NO ...'

The Dance of Death

1

The Music City dance hall was lit up as usual with spotlights focussed on various areas of the dancefloor. The hall was decorated to enthuse and invigorate the dancers who gathered there each week for their regular evening of dancing and music.

James had been going along to these dances, on and off, for around two or three years now. Tonight, he had been up and dancing along with all the others to the sounds that filled the hall. Now, he was sat at his table watching the bodies gyrating around to the music being played from the stage to his right-hand side by a couple of the regular DJs. They, too, were adding to the atmosphere and complementing the proceedings with their upbeat patter and personality. The whole room was bouncing with the beat of the music.

The highlight of these evenings each week was known as "The Last Dance". Usually a slow dance, but not exclusively. Also, it was aimed to be a romantic dance for those who wanted to get a little closer at the end of the evening.

Emily had been sat at the next table to James. She had been dancing throughout the evening with various groups of people, including James.

Tonight, Emily was ready for The Last Dance. She looked over towards James. He beckoned her to join him on the dance floor. She smiled back and nodded. They both rose from their seats and met each other on the way to the dance floor.

'I always enjoy The Last Dance. Don't you, James?' Emily said.

'Yes, it's a great way to get to know someone. Shall we find a space? I think there's one over here.' James pointed at an area near where they had both been sitting. As they moved closer, they took hold of each other and the music began.

Emily began gyrating around whilst holding James. He looked down at her movements.

'Don't look at my feet, James. Look into my eyes.'

James smiled. He remembered back when he had taken dance lessons the instructors would often tell the dancers to focus on their partner in front of them and not down at their feet.

Emily held James a little tighter. Then loosened her grip to repeat her words. 'Focus on my eyes, James.'

He looked deep into her eyes. They were even more mesmerising than watching her body writhing to the music.

'Are you focussing on my eyes now?'

'Yes, Emily.' James was transfixed.

James felt her grip appear to tighten, then loosen again a few times until he began to feel a little giddy.

'Keep focussing on my eyes.' Emily stared back at James. He was taller than her, but her heeled dancing shoes minimised their height difference.

'Do you like my eyes, James?'

He nodded.

'Are they beautiful, James?'

'Yes. They are beautiful.'

'Keep focussing on my beautiful eyes.'

'So beautiful.'

She began to run her hands rhythmically through his hair and massaged his temples gently. Then she pulled James even closer to her whilst maintaining their eye contact. His body mirrored her movements.

They continued dancing like this until the dance ended.

'I think we need to go home now, James. Don't you?'

'Yes.'

'Shall we go home?'

'Yes. Let's go home.'

Emily put her arm around James as they left the club and they went over to her car. He got into the passenger seat. She drove. They headed back to her place.

2

Emily had been going to these dances for a few years now. She enjoyed meeting up with friends, listening to the music and dancing. She also enjoyed the fact that they took place at Music City on a Sunday night and lots of people met up, socialised, made friends and had a good time.

However, life changed for her the night she went home with Fyson.

He was a tall, athletically built man about the same age as Emily and he was a fantastic dancer. Many of the women at these dances wanted to dance with him and he would, more often than not, oblige.

The night he took Emily back to his place he had danced with her on and off throughout the evening. Inevitably, when The Last Dance came, they danced it together.

When the evening was over, he suggested they went back to his place for a drink. She smiled and agreed. They left together.

When they arrived at his home, Fyson went into the kitchen to get some drinks while Emily remained in the lounge. She was looking at some ornaments he had on a cabinet at one side of the room as he returned with their drinks.

'These look really nice.' She pointed at the ornaments. He put his arm around her and planting a kiss on her cheek smiled at her and said, 'Yes, but you are gorgeous.'

She smiled. 'Thanks.'

He kissed her again this time on the lips and much more meaningfully. She felt it was a little inappropriate given they had only come back for a post dance drink but he continued to hold her in his arms.

Fyson grabbed her by the waist. Tightly. He pulled her into his body and they kissed some more. The longer they kissed the more passionate the kissing became. Emily had enjoyed the initial kisses but now was beginning to feel concerned. She resisted but his strength was overpowering. He was so strong and he was reaching a point where she was feeling very uncomfortablc. She tried to push him away and create some space but he wouldn't relinquish his tight embrace. He was so strong.

He pushed her backwards. She didn't realise it but she had been standing by the end of the sofa. She went over and flat out onto the sofa. He followed on top of her. She let out a short sharp scream as she fell but then froze as he continued and began removing her clothing. Her mind was racing but her body paralysed with her legs draped over the edge of the sofa.

He went on to have sex with her. She was frozen with fear but screaming inside. She had closed her eyes but couldn't stop her tears falling slowly from them as the ordeal continued. He gripped her tight and spoke quietly but breathlessly. 'You don't need to shut your eyes, babe. You have beautiful eyes. You shouldn't close them. I want to see your lovely eyes.'

She wasn't listening. She was still paralysed with terror. He continued to rape her. She had no idea how long this lasted as she had lost all track of time. When it was over, he left the room. She remained frozen for a brief while then started sobbing. Yet, inside, she felt her anger rising too.

She finally managed to summon up the strength to get up off of the sofa. She grabbed her bag which was lying a short distance away on the floor and rummaged inside it. She wasn't sure what she was looking for until she spotted some tablets. Sleeping tablets, she thought. So grabbing a handful of them she leant over and dropped them into his drink can sat on a table beside her.

When he returned, she was kneeling on the floor beside the table where his drink was and where her bag had settled. She was shaking with fear.

He smiled.

She started to panic and went to get up.

He pushed her back down on the floor, forced himself on her and had sex with her again. Emily did not speak. Any remaining strength she had had gone after trying to fight him off earlier.

Eventually, Fyson got up off of her and picked up his drink and tipped it back in one go as if in smug celebration at this conquest.

She dropped to the floor. Her eyes still closed. She began to weep again. Then finding some effort, hauled herself to her feet and ran away. Unfortunately, only into a small utility room. She paused in panic. She looked around terrified she may be trapped but he had not followed.

She turned and raced back out to look for the front door. Running into the lounge she froze again when she saw him on the floor in front of her. He wasn't moving. She wondered if he was asleep.

She was standing outside his bedroom door and spotted some pillows on his bed. Grabbing one of them she ran over to where he lay. Then she pressed it hard over his face. He didn't move.

She knelt on the pillow, occasionally pressing harder to make sure it was completely covering him. Her anger dissipating as she continued to smother his face. Some time passed. No movement. She regained some of her senses, grabbed her bag and ran out into the street and home.

3

Several months passed before Emily met up with anyone from Music City. During this time, she discovered that she had changed. She had developed a bitter but more cautious attitude towards any man that she encountered. It had affected her mental attitude so that she would be very uncomfortable when in a situation close to a man. Emily would feel threatened but had developed a hardness which manifested itself by her lack of concern about the man and focussed solely on protecting herself in situations where she felt that threat. She had avowed never to put herself in that kind of vulnerable position ever again.

She had gone over the events of that night at Fyson's house in her mind many times and come to a number of different conclusions. The ones that stayed with her included: why had she allowed herself to be carried away by his charm in such a way that her defences had lowered so much by agreeing to go back to Fyson's in the first place, and why had she not behaved differently, been more forceful and not given him cause to believe that she would be happy with his actions? She blamed herself. But she vowed that nothing like that would ever happen to her again. She would have to take control in future. She also felt that she could have used her training in hypnosis to control the situation better. She might try that in the future too.

Several months after that night she bumped into Clara, a friend from Music City, whilst on her way home from the shops.

'Emily!' Clara called over to her.

Emily turned around and spotted Clara immediately. They met and embraced.

'Where have you been, Em?' Clara enquired, 'we haven't seen you at the Sunday Club for ages.'

'I've been very busy. I decided to have a break. I've been on holiday.'

'You must come along, Em. We are all missing you.'

'Aw. That's sweet, Clara. Perhaps I will.'

They talked for several minutes and as they talked Emily realised that she was missing the social aspect of the evening and her other friends too. When they parted, Clara's inspiring words had persuaded Emily that it was time for her to return.

She made an arrangement with Clara that she would go along to Music City the following Sunday. Clara would pick her up from home and they would leave early.

And that is what they did.

Emily thought a lot about her returning in the days

following the meeting with Clara. Eventually, she made a firm decision that, in future, if a lift in Clara's car wasn't available, she would take her own car and if she took anyone home, they would go back to her place so that she could be in control. She also decided to give the hypnosis idea a try to see if it would work on someone in the dance environment in the same way as it did when she used it at her work.

4

One Sunday night, with Clara not around, she met Tony and decided it was time to put some of her ideas into practice. When Emily danced with Tony it was earlier in the evening and not The Last Dance so she thought it would be a good time just to give the hypnosis idea a try in the dancing environment and see if it would enable her to take control.

When she tried it out, she discovered Tony was particular susceptible, he went under her influence really quickly and seemingly quite deeply. It scared her a little and she brought him out of it after a very short time. It did prove it was possible in a noisy, bustling dance hall though. She did conclude that Tony was probably someone who was easy to put under and other subjects might be more of a challenge. Nevertheless, it made her feel a little more confident about taking someone back to her place in the future.

It was some weeks later when Emily met Jayden. He asked her for The Last Dance. She agreed.

Jayden had wandering hands. A fact that Emily didn't realise before agreeing to dance with him. She became more and more irritated by finding herself having to deal with his hands constantly drifting to intimate parts of her body. She snapped and decided she would make him pay for his actions.

She began her response by fixing her gaze on him and suggesting he did too. She tried to speak to him to get some control. Although it didn't seem to work at first, she persevered and eventually as the dance ended, she felt it had been successful.

She suggested he walked over to the other side of the hall and back to test if she now had control of him. He obeyed her commands completely and then returned to her.

'I want you, Emily,' he said as they reconnected their gaze.

'You don't want me, Jayden,' she replied calmly.

'I do. I want you.'

'Listen to me, Jayden.' She paused. Now she would take full control 'Are you listening?'

'Yes.'

'Repeat this, Jayden.' She paused again. He was still with her. She held him tightly. 'I want.'

'I want.'

'I want to go.'

'I want to go.'

'I want to go home.'

'I want to go home.' He repeated her words robotically.

'Say it again, Jayden.'

'I want...to go home.'

'You want to go home, Jayden.'

'I want to go home.'

OK, Jayden. Let's go home.'

OK.'

'When I say, "Let's go home" we will walk to my car. You will get in the passenger seat. We will go home.' Another pause. OK. Do you understand, Jayden?'

OK.'

'So, what do you want, Jayden?'

'I want to go home.'

'Let's go home.'

Emily took his hand and they walked out to her car. She took him home.

By the end of the evening, he had paid for his behaviour earlier and Emily was pleased with the way everything turned out.

5

As Emily and James arrived back at her home, she prepared to put her plan into action. She had used it before with Jayden, amongst others, and now had it well-rehearsed.

She parked up outside her house and they both stepped out of the car. She walked around to the pavement where James was now standing. They held hands and walked into the house.

Once inside she led him through a small hallway and into the lounge.

'James.'

'Yes.'

She pointed at one of the armchairs in her lounge. 'Go over to that armchair and sit down.'

OK.'

He walked over to the armchair and sat down just as she had instructed.

'How are you feeling, James?'

OK.'

'Are you comfortable in the chair?'

'Yes.'

'Would you like a drink, James?'

'Yes, please.'

'Would you like a strong coffee, James?'

'OK.'

At that point Emily disappeared into the kitchen and began to prepare their drinks. A glass of white wine for herself and a strong coffee for James. As she made James's coffee, she picked up a small container from the back of one of her cupboards and added the liquid inside it into James's drink. It was something she had researched specifically for this sort of occasion since her encounter with Fyson some time back.

With the drinks made and the coffee spiked she emerged back into the lounge with his coffee in her hand and walked over to where James was sitting.

'It's my very special coffee blend, James. Do make sure you drink it all so you can enjoy the flavour properly. You will drink it all won't you James.'

'Yes.'

She sat down in another armchair and continued to talk to him, making sure he was still under her spell. Her voice was purposefully controlled and the replies James gave continued to be brief and compliant.

After a short while she pointed to his cup of coffee. 'James, I think you should drink your coffee now. Don't you? You must be very thirsty. It's been a long tiring evening.'

'OK.'

He drank the coffee. He managed to drink it all in two large swigs from the cup.

Satisfied with James's response, Emily rose from the chair and left the room. She went to the kitchen where she had left her wine and tidied up a little whilst sipping her drink.

Once she had finished it was time to return to the lounge. She stopped and looked back at the kitchen worktop and decided to wash up their drinks first and then call it a night.

When she returned to the lounge James was motionless in the armchair.

She removed the cup from his hand and placed it on a nearby table. Then reaching over behind the armchair, drew up a large woollen throw. This she draped carefully across the armchair ensuring it covered James completely.

As she moved across the room, picking up the cup and heading towards the kitchen, she saw her suitcases by the doorway. She would have to pack them up for her holiday tomorrow. The first thing she needed to do in the morning would be to deal with the body.

The Witch's Daughter

1

> *Who is the girl from the house on the hill?*
>
> *They say she is evil; they say she will kill*
>
> *But I know that I love her and I always will*
>
> *Who is the girl from the house on the hill?*

Jenkin Bulcock found himself on the busy motorway and seemingly heading towards a major traffic snarl up. All around him vehicles were already beginning to slow down and the information he was receiving from his Sat Nav suggested that not so many miles away, the road was blocked and everything was at a standstill.

Fortunately, Jenkin had been this way before and he knew a way around this problem. A cut through. It would take him down what would be deserted country lanes and into the desolate moorland that was a feature of the area. But it would be away from the motorway traffic.

He turned off. A number of other cars did so too but they had other places to go. His route took him way off the beaten track through a couple of sleepy villages and over the high moors to re-join the traffic, hopefully, far beyond the motorway jam. He would only need a short detour after that to take him back to his original route.

But it was getting dark. In the distance a mist was visible and appeared to be getting denser as he continued his journey.

A couple of quick turns on his route and he was heading through the village of Shawburn. This would take him past Shawburn Fell and up over the high moor.

As the car headed up a small lane out of the village, the road began to climb upwards. The further up he went, so the fog closed in around until the visibility had dropped down to just a few yards. Jenkin peered through the condensation forming on his windscreen as he tried to make out the road ahead. He slowed the car down, that led to the engine stalling and the car stopped. He slammed on the brake and handbrake as it began to roll backwards and came to a full stop.

He tried to restart the car but the engine refused to start. He tried again but still no luck.

Suddenly, he was startled by a dark shape passing in front of his car bonnet. It was like a large black shadow. He stared out into the swirling fog.

Increasingly concerned, he decided to get out of the car and check the engine.

As he approached the bonnet, he sensed someone or something moving nearby.

'Hello,' he called out. 'Anybody there?'

A large black shape reared up behind him ...

2

The following morning, as the fog cleared, the village was buzzing with the news of an incident on the high moor. People were gathering in and around the Village Store.

Since dawn, all sorts of traffic had been passing through the village: an ambulance, police cars, vans and a variety of other vehicles. It disturbed the normally quiet routine of life in the village.

'I heard there's been a body found up on the hill near Old Bessie Craddock's. You know, on the high moor,' one villager told a fellow neighbour.

'I know. I heard it was a stranger. They found him dead. Must have lost himself in the fog last night, I expect.'

'You know, if you look carefully up the lane, you can make out the activity up by Bessie Craddock's cottage. You can just about see it through the mist on the moor.'

They both stared intently towards where the vehicles had gathered.

Outside the cottage, Detective Inspector Jim Hargreaves was trying to peer through a dirty windowpane and into the cottage. His sergeant was doing the same thing at a nearby window.

The inspector drew his finger across the glass and held it up to his colleague. 'Look at this window. It's filthy!'

Sergeant Holt had spotted a cloth on the ground. He picked it up and tried to wipe the dirt off of the window. The cloth wasn't particularly clean so it made very little difference. He pressed his face against the slightly cleaner patch of glass, jumping back in shock as a large black dog reared up to the other side of the glass and began barking loudly and salivating on the window.

Hargreaves smiled. 'What's up? Has someone attacked you?'

Sergeant Holt regained his composure. 'It's OK. I was startled by the dog jumping up at the window. It just startled me for a moment, that's all.'

The inspector continued smiling and moved closer to his colleague, as Holt approached the window again. This time more slowly. The dog continued barking, jumping up and rattling the window as it did so. He looked inside as best he could through the dirt.

'I don't think anyone is in.' Sergeant Holt tried to clear a little more grime away whilst the dog inside became increasingly more agitated.

'Possibly not,' Hargreaves replied barely audibly. 'Let's try later. Perhaps the dog owner might be back by then and you can get better acquainted with it.' He smiled at his colleague but Holt didn't respond to the teasing.

They both started back to their car. The dog's barking still reverberating from inside the house.

'It was pretty dark in there,' Sergeant Holt said. 'I could hardly see anything clearly. I couldn't see much lighting in the room.'

They drove off in the car. 'Perhaps we'll see if any of the villagers can shed some light on what happened,' Inspector Hargreaves said, staring thoughtfully out of the window. 'Didn't I see a pub in the village? There's bound to be something we can pick up in there.'

Holt smiled wryly at the comment. He suspected it might be an excuse for picking up more than just information.

Hargreaves continued, 'It is thirsty work, after all!'

3

Hargreaves and Holt walked into the main bar of the Frog and Snake. It was an old-style village pub with a number of locals sitting at their tables, drinks in front of them. One or two of them looked up as the two strangers entered.

They approached the bar and were greeted at the counter by one of the bar staff. 'Evening gentlemen,' he said.

'Evening,' Hargreaves responded. 'I'm Detective Inspector Hargreaves and this is my colleague, Detective Sergeant Holt. Can we speak to the Manager, please?'

'I'm the manager here along with my sister, Tess.' He pointed towards the back room of the pub. 'My name's Jake. We are joint licensees here. I suppose you've come about the body they've found up by Old Bessie Craddock's cottage.'

'We need to ask some questions about what you may have seen. Have you noticed anything unusual around the area since last night?'

Jake shook his head. 'I was working in here last night. I couldn't really see anything outside.' He pointed over towards the frosted windows in the bar. 'It was fairly quiet in here last night. Just a few regulars in. The weather was pretty awful. Very foggy.'

'What about your sister? Might she have seen anything?' Hargreaves asked.

'It's possible. She was upstairs most of the time. Our living area is above the bar.' Jake looked up to the ceiling before returning his gaze to Inspector Hargreaves. 'Shall I call her over?'

Hargreaves nodded.

Tess had been looking inquisitively into the bar whilst busying herself in the back room. Jake beckoned her over. She acknowledged his wave.

'So, have you found anything up on the moor like folks say?' Jake enquired.

'We're still investigating,' Hargreaves replied.

Sergeant Holt was looking around the bar, occasionally taking interest in the discussion.

Jake's sister appeared from the back room. Jake turned to her 'It's the police, Tess. They're asking about last night.'

Tess walked over and spoke to Hargreaves and Holt. 'I was upstairs watching the telly.'

Hargreaves was deep in thought. 'Did you see anything unusual outside last night?' he asked.

'Not really. It was quite foggy, and I was sitting at the back so couldn't really see anything out front.'

'You didn't look out front at all?'

'Not really. I'm sure I went to the front window at some point during the evening, but it was too foggy to see anything.'

'Did something disturb you? Was there a reason that you went to the window?'

'No. I don't think so. Perhaps a programme had ended, or something like that and I just walked over.' She paused. 'I think it was whilst I was getting myself a drink. Yes, that was it. I was waiting for the kettle to boil and just peered out through the mist. That's all.'

'I see.' Hargreaves looked over to his colleague who gestured towards some customers. 'Do you mind if we question some of your customers?'

Tess shrugged. 'No, of course not. Go ahead,'

Jake said, 'The two old gentlemen at the corner table often know all there is to know about the goings-on in the village. You could try them. The one with a beard is known as Old Growcher and his friend we call Rumbling Pete Bogg. He might be able to help.'

'Thanks.' Turning to Sergeant Holt he pointed over to the other customers. 'You see what you can find out from them. I'll speak to these two.' He gestured at the two customers Jake had spoken about.

'OK.'

Jake called to Inspector Hargreaves and his colleague. 'Would you like a drink whilst you're here?'

Hargreaves looked over to Holt. 'Just a coffee, if it's

possible.'

'OK. No problem,' Jake replied.

Holt nodded. 'Just a fruit juice for me.'

'Orange, pineapple, lemon—?'

'An orange juice will be fine,' Holt said.

Jake acknowledged this and went off to prepare their drinks.

Inspector Hargreaves went over to where the two gentlemen were sitting and introduced himself. 'Evening gentlemen. My name's Detective Inspector Hargreaves.' The younger of the two held his hand out in greeting.

'Peter Boggins.' They shook hands. He gestured to Inspector Hargreaves to sit down. His bearded companion looked on suspiciously. 'What can we do for you?' Boggins asked helpfully.

'We're asking around the village whether anyone saw anything unusual around the area last night, or perhaps this morning.'

Boggins shook his head. 'No. Nothing.' He turned to his companion, who was quietly sipping a pint of beer. 'Did you see anything?'

He creased up his eyes, scowled under his bushy beard and shook his head.

'No. We've not seen anything.' Boggins turned back to Hargreaves. 'We were both in here last night 'till quite late. It was very foggy out, y'know.'

Finally, the bearded man spoke. 'Some folks say the fog was a spell cast by the Witch.'

Hargreaves was a little taken aback. 'Who says?'

'Some folks.' He returned to his pint.

'Sorry I didn't catch your name.'

Boggins intervened. 'There's a village superstition that Old Bessie Craddock has cursed the village and this bad weather is her doing. Last night's fog was another chance for them to repeat the nonsense.'

'It's not nonsense. The village is cursed. The Witch cursed it,' Old Growcher growled.

Hargreaves looked on in disbelief. He picked up the conversation. 'Who is this witch then?'

'Old Bessie Craddock,' Boggins said, 'they say she's a Witch. They call her home "The Witch's Cottage".'

Hargreaves shook his head in disbelief. He turned to the bearded man again. 'What is your name?'

The man remained tight-lipped.

'His name is Tom Bunn,' Boggins said helpfully. 'We call him Old Growcher.' The two of them exchanged disapproving glances.

Tom Bunn sneered a little then, pointing a finger at Inspector Hargreaves, before speaking slowly and deliberately. 'They say it's the Witch's doing. Her, her daughter and that evil dog.'

Boggins smiled at Hargreaves who was now slightly open mouthed. 'Don't take him too seriously. Old

Growcher is always grumbling about something.'

'Have you found a body?' Tom Bunn said, continuing his belligerent manner.

'Why do you ask?'

'They say you found a body.'

Boggins smiled back at Hargreaves weakly and shrugged his shoulders. 'There's been a lot of talk around the village today. Gossip y'know. People imagine things. I doubt anyone could have seen anything, though. It was too foggy. As I say, they imagine things. All sorts of things. No, they can't have seen anything. Not really.'

Hargreaves picked up the coffee that had arrived and drank it thoughtfully. 'Has anyone in the village gone missing recently? Perhaps up on the moor, for instance.'

They both shook their heads.

'No one has seen Old Bessie Craddock for a while but her daughter, Katrina, is going out with one of the lads from the village. They are often about. Not in today, though.' Boggins looked around the bar as he spoke. 'Perhaps they could help you.'

Hargreaves finished his drink. 'What's the lad's name?'

'Bobby Duckworth. He lives at his parents' place. It's the store on the corner opposite. You can't miss it it's even called "The Village Store".'

'Thanks. We may pay them a visit.'

Sergeant Holt returned. Hargreaves shook hands again with Peter Boggins whilst his friend continued to scowl. Then waving over to Jake and Tess at the bar they left and decided to call it a day.

Back in their car and heading out of the village, Hargreaves finally spoke as Holt drove. 'We'll see what information uniform may have uncovered back at the office tomorrow. Then we may need to have another go at this cottage. Perhaps we need to check if anyone's picked up anything about the people at The Village Store at the same time.'

'OK.'

'We'll call it a night.'

4

Hargreaves walked into his office closely followed by Holt. He sat down and Holt sat opposite.

'So, what have we got so far?' he said.

Holt began flicking through a file of papers. 'I have picked up some paperwork from uniform. They are processing it at the moment. They've interviewed a number of the residents in Shawburn but I don't think they've come up with anything usable.'

'Did they manage to speak to the Craddocks?'

'No sir.'

Hargreaves nodded his head and creased his face up in a manner that conveyed his displeasure. 'Well first things first. We will need to interview Mrs Craddock and her daughter, Katrina.'

'Yes sir.'

'They can't have simply vanished. They must be around somewhere. If they can't help us and there's nothing further from uniform on the ground then there's nothing further that we can do either.'

Holt continued to flick through the copies of the reports. Hargreaves peered across the desk and enquired 'Found anything?'

'Not really, sir. Uniform have spoken to a lot of the villagers but as I say the information is rather sketchy and not particularly helpful.'

'There're not many people in the village anyway. Did anyone say anything at all?'

'Not about the night in question. There's a lot of, well, kind of wild and somewhat bizarre stuff from other times though.'

Hargreaves looked unimpressed. 'Like what?'

'Well, here, for example. A villager says they saw a large black panther like creature silhouetted by the horizon just after sunset. When asked when they saw this they replied, "perhaps a few weeks back".'

'Here, let me see this.' Holt handed the report across the desk and Hargreaves began perusing through the notes. 'I see what you mean. This isn't going to be any help at all.' He paused then restarted. 'What's this here?' He pointed at one of the sheets. 'It says someone reported seeing Bessie Craddock's daughter turn into a wild cat! It's laughable.'

Holt took up the point. 'There's another couple of comments where the villagers accuse the Craddocks of being witches and shapeshifters.'

'Shape what?'

'Shapeshifters, sir,' Holt said. 'I did some research into it. It's where people are able to transform themselves into different animals and back into human form.'

Hargreaves looked astonished at his colleague's remarks. 'Really.'

Holt thought he'd better explain. 'I thought if the villagers really believe in this stuff, it might be helpful to understand what they are suggesting that they've seen. What they are accusing the Craddocks of doing.'

'I see,' Hargreaves replied. 'I just remember what that man in the Frog and Snake said though. One of the ones I spoke to. Pete Boggins. He said no-one could really have seen anything on the night because of the fog. Whatever they are coming up with here is just their vivid imaginations. It seems to me that their minds are playing tricks on them.'

A silence followed whilst Hargreaves went through the rest of the reports. The two of them read through them occasionally swapping paperwork as they did so.

Eventually, Hargreaves broke the silence. 'We need to focus on the matter at hand. We need to identify if it was a wild animal that did this and whether anyone else was involved? It's Mr Bulcock's death we are investigating. A lot of this is noise. If there is a wild animal loose on the high moor, we can pass that information on to the relevant agency. If not ... well, we'll see. Meantime we need to speak to the Craddocks so we can, hopefully, eliminate them.'

Holt nodded in agreement.

The office door opened and a constable peered into the office. 'Sir, there's someone at the desk asking to speak to you.'

'Who is it, Constable?'

'It's a Katrina Craddock. She says you were looking for her.'

Hargreaves and Holt glanced at each other open mouthed. Hargreaves broke the brief silence. 'Show her into the Interview room, Constable. We'll be along shortly.'

'Sir.'

5

The two detectives headed for the Interview room and walked in. Across the room, standing side by side, was a man and a woman. Hargreaves beckoned them to sit at the seats by the table in the centre of the room. He then took a seat opposite alongside Holt.

'Good afternoon,' Hargreaves greeted them studying them both intensely. 'I am Detective Inspector Hargreaves and this is Detective Sergeant Holt. Can you confirm your names for us?'

The woman spoke. 'I am Katrina Craddock. This is Bobby, Bobby Duckworth. He says that he'd heard you have been trying to track me down to speak me.' Bobby nodded.

'Someone in the village told me,' Bobby said quietly.

Hargreaves focussed his gaze on the woman. She was older than Bobby, possibly by ten to fifteen years he reckoned. She wore her dark hair long, draped over her shoulders and down her back. Her piercing eyes were a deep brown colour and her lipstick applied liberally; a glossy red.

Katrina took up the conversation. 'We were in town so I thought I would come in and save you the trouble of looking for me.' She stared back at Hargreaves in a way that he found unsettling. He decided this was her way of trying to intimidate him. He had known far more, often very disturbed, criminals try far worse.

'We've been trying to locate your mother: Mrs Elizabeth Craddock.' Hargreaves said unfazed by her attitude.

'It's Bessie Craddock,' Katrina responded tersely.

'Do you know where we can find her?'

'She's at home.'

'I see. Well, we need to speak to her. Is there a good time we can perhaps call round to ask her some questions?'

'She doesn't speak to strangers.'

'She'll have to speak to us,' Hargreaves insisted, staring back at Katrina. She shrugged her shoulders.

'OK, let's talk about yourself. Where were you the evening before last? It was a particularly foggy night.'

Katrina paused in a way meant to convey she was ignoring the question after the discussion about her mother. After a brief silence she finally responded. 'I was out.'

'And where were you exactly?'

'If you must know I was with Bobby.' She indicated towards her boyfriend sitting quietly beside her.

He looked back at her and then turned to the two detectives. 'That's right. She was with me.'

'And where were you both?'

'I was with him at his home in the village.'

'At The Village Store.'

'Yes.'

'All night.'

'Yes, all night.'

Bobby nodded.

'Did you return home the following morning?' Hargreaves said, whilst Holt scribbled notes of the conversation.

'No, not then.' Katrina looked over to Bobby. 'We both went off into town in the morning. We didn't get back until later in the day.'

'So, when did you return home?'

'I went home in the evening. Around seven, I think.'

'The following day?' She nodded. Hargreaves sought further clarification. 'Yesterday.' She nodded again.

'Was your mother home?'

Slightly irritated by the question Katrina slowly replied, 'As I told you, she's always home.'

'She wasn't there when we called yesterday. All we saw was the dog.'

'That was Balor. He looks after the house. Keeps prying eyes away.'

'But no sign of your mother.'

Now more irritated Katrina responded forcefully. 'I told you. She's always there.'

'We are going to have to speak to your mother.'

'As I said she won't speak to you.'

'And as I said, she will have to speak to us. Will she be in tomorrow?'

Katrina rolled her eyes and looked exasperated. 'You'll be wasting your time.'

'Will she be there?'

'Of course.' Katrina's tone revealing her frustration at the question.

'Good. Then we'll call in tomorrow to speak to her.'

Katrina shrugged her shoulders again. 'She won't be able to help.'

'Perhaps not.' Hargreaves smiled in a manner that betrayed his own feelings at Katrina's attitude. 'We'll see. We need to find out what she may or may not know about the incident. We'll be round tomorrow.'

He waved towards the door and Holt, putting down his pen and notes, stood up and proceeded to lead Katrina and Bobby out of the office.

6

Hargreaves had been home only five to ten minutes when his phone rang. It was Holt.

'Sir, there's been another incident in Shawburn.'

'Oh, what is it? What's happened?'

'We've just received a call. It appears a group of villagers are heading up to The Witch's Cottage intending to burn it down.'

'They're doing what!' Hargreaves stared out of a nearby window in astonishment. 'What do they think this is? Some kind of seventeenth century witch hunt or something!'

Holt followed up his colleague's comments. 'I know. It's crazy. I'm on my way there now. Our information is that the other emergency services are also on their way too.'

'OK. Thanks.'

'I should be arriving there in about ten to fifteen minutes.'

'Great.' Hargreaves was already heading towards his front door. 'I'll meet up with you there.'

Hargreaves headed out to his car and drove off towards Shawburn. It took him a little over half an hour to get there and as he turned onto the lane by the village green, he noticed Holt's car parked at the roadside. He pulled up behind the vehicle. Looking out over the green, he spotted Holt outside The Village Store. He appeared to be talking to someone at the upstairs window.

His colleague spotted him and began to walk over. Hargreaves rolled his window down. 'What's happening?' he asked. He noticed as the outside air began to fill the car it was heavy with smoke fumes billowing down from the moor.

Holt approached the car. 'It's Katrina Craddock, sir.' He pointed back towards the Store. Hargreaves could make out a figure peering out of the upstairs window and looking up the hill towards the incident. 'I was just speaking to her. She's with Bobby. She's quite rattled, sir. Not the calm, controlled Katrina we interviewed earlier.'

'I expect not. Isn't she worried about her mother?'

'She seemed more concerned about her own situation, to be honest. She said her mother would be fine. The dog would be fine too!'

Hargreaves pointed up towards the cottage. 'So, they haven't burned the Craddock's cottage down then?'

'No sir. I was up there as soon as I arrived. It seems that there was some kind of accident that occurred before they arrived at the cottage. The fire brigade is dealing with it.'

'OK.' Hargreaves said. 'Let's get up there then and catch up with the latest developments.'

'OK, sir. I'll follow you up.'

Hargreaves drove the short distance to where the emergency vehicles were parked. Two police vehicles had blocked the lane off at either end and cordoned the area off from the village. A couple of ambulances were in attendance as well as a fire tender. Although any flames had been extinguished, there was still lots of smoke around and firemen dampening down the area by the gates to the Cottage.

Leaving his car, Hargreaves walked over to where a couple of constables were standing. They were talking to some of the villagers. One of two of whom were already drifting away and back to the village. Holt joined him.

'So, what's happened?' Hargreaves asked addressing the constable nearest to him.

The constable pointed towards the gate. 'It seems someone was a little careless. They spilt some fuel they were carrying and a nearby spark set it alight.'

'Before they got to the main house?'

'Yes.' The constable continued the story. 'There were three villagers at the head of the group. They have been burnt by the ensuing blaze. The ambulance crew have already put them onto their vehicles ready to take them away.'

'Are they badly burned?'

'Not really, sir. One of them is worse than the other two. It seems it's mainly burns to the lower body. Their feet and legs. The more serious one also has burns to his hands and arms.'

Holt chipped in pointing at Mrs Craddock's cottage. 'They don't seem to have got anywhere near the house then.'

The constable shook his head.

'Quite,' Hargreaves replied.

The other constable joined the conversation. 'The villagers are pretty spooked by it all. They are saying it's witchcraft.'

Hargreaves rolled his eyes dismissively and shook his head.

A villager walking past overheard the tail end of the constable's comments. 'It is witchcraft. Old Bessie Craddock has brought nothing but trouble to this village. She has cursed us all.'

He wandered off muttering first back to them and then to himself.

'Have you checked the house?' Hargreaves said to the two constables.

'Yes. It's empty. Oh, apart from the dog. He seems to be fairly lively. Though seemingly unaffected by the goings-on out here.'

'No sign of anyone at all?'

'No. Just the dog.'

Hargreaves turned back to Holt. 'I wonder where the elusive Bessie Craddock is then.' Holt shrugged his shoulders. 'If there's nothing further that we can do here we may as well head back.'

'OK, sir.'

'Leave the tidying up to uniform.'

The two constables walked off towards the other emergency vehicles.

'Shall I catch you up on everything in the morning then, sir?' Holt enquired.

'Yes. Do that. I'll see you back at the station tomorrow.'

7

Hargreaves arrived in the office that morning slightly later than he had anticipated after a particularly long meeting. As he approached, he noticed Holt staring as if transfixed by his computer screen. He stopped in his tracks and side-stepped over towards his colleague's desk.

Holt was now looking down at some papers as Hargreaves reached the desk. He returned to staring at the screen.

'So, what's new?' Hargreaves looked down at where Holt was seated.

Holt turned his head slowly to meet the gaze of Hargreaves.

'Sir, the first forensics have come through on the Bulcock death.'

'OK. So, what do we know?'

'Also, I've received some other information. Documents about Mrs Craddock.'

Hargreaves nodded. 'And ...'

'Well, we have obtained DNA records from a cold case Mrs Craddock was involved in a few years back. The case isn't related but the DNA is.'

'OK.'

'Forensics have managed to extract DNA from the crime scene. From the scratches on the paintwork on the bonnet of Bulcock's car.' Holt paused and looked up to a silent Hargreaves. 'There's a DNA match with Mrs Craddock from that cold case.'

Hargreaves did a double take. 'Really. So, Bessie Craddock is involved in the Bulcock death.'

'Possibly not.'

'But you said ... the DNA ...' Hargreaves pointed at Holt's desk as if the DNA was somehow present on it.

'The thing is, sir. I've also got a death certificate here from a couple of years back.'

Holt picked up a document and offered it to Hargreaves. He took it and began reading it. He then looked back to Holt. 'It's Mrs Craddock's death certificate.'

Holt nodded and took the document back. 'Yes sir.'

'She's dead,' Hargreaves said incredulously.

'Yes sir. But there's more.'

'More! How can she be more than dead?'

'More forensics sir.' Holt returned to his screen and began tapping on his keyboard. He stopped and pointed at the screen. 'According to forensics they also tested the scratches, cuts and gashes on Bulcock's body.'

Hargreaves craned over to look at the screen.

'They also found traces of hair. Or maybe fur from

what could be a cat-like animal. Possibly something like a cougar or, more likely, a puma. That sort of thing. Anyway, a wild cat.'

Hargreaves took a step back and shook his head in disbelief. 'Wait a minute. Are we saying that the forensics is telling us that Mrs Craddock and a wild cat killed Bulcock?'

Holt shook his head.

'You're not on your shapeshifter nonsense from the other day. Are you?'

Once again, he shook his head.

'No sir. I know that if it were plausible, it might be an explanation. And if people really believe in that sort of thing that might be the conclusion they would draw.'

'You mean like the villagers.'

'Exactly.'

'So, Mrs Craddock has not turned into some sort of zombie shapeshifter then. Well, I'm relieved to hear it.'

'No sir.' Holt paused.

'So, what have we got then?'

'Let's assume a wild cat killed Bulcock. But the fact is the DNA on Bulcock's body is not Mrs Craddock's. But it is a close relative.'

'Her daughter?'

'Yes sir. Her daughter, Katrina.'

Road to Redemption

1

Maria was carrying two bags and a kitchen knife. Her handbag was slung over one shoulder and a small suitcase-type bag across her other shoulder. Her right hand had a firm grip on the knife. She strode purposefully into the darkness.

She walked briskly down the garden path, out of the back gate and into the alleyway that ran behind the houses.

She made her way along to the end of the alley and into the road that led down to the riverside. There she joined the towpath and headed out into the night.

This break free from her husband was pre-planned. She had thought it would happen sooner rather than later. It was happening now. Maria had often spoken about the situation with trusted friends. So now she was determined to make it work, despite the hardship it was likely to bring her. It did promise a very different life and an uncertain future. But it would be a future free from his abuse. That alone was worth this ordeal.

After walking for around three or four miles, she began to calm herself down. Her mind was starting to focus on organising the thoughts that had been circling around in her head. The first thing to deal with was the kitchen knife that was still in her right hand. She needed to get rid of it. Walking on a few paces, she turned towards the river and hurled it into the centre of the water. She watched it disappear. Maria continued on.

The bruise on her left cheek was also beginning to hurt. She touched it gently with her hand and winced in pain. Although it was tender, Maria needed to focus on putting as much distance as she could between herself and him as fast as possible. She picked up her pace.

A couple of hours passed by and tiredness was becoming a real problem too. A little further on she found a small riverside bench. It would be an ideal place to stop and rest. Unfortunately, the rest gave her dark thoughts a chance to overwhelm her again and that, coupled with the pain from her cheek and her aching limbs, was too much; she started to cry.

Nevertheless, Maria knew she had to press on. Dawn was no more than an hour or two away. So, pulling herself together again, she stood up from the seat, dried her eyes, and with a renewed strength of purpose, continued to walk on towards the sunrise.

By the time dawn broke, Maria had paused a few more times to rest from her increasing weariness. Looking over to the horizon it was possible to see the resort town of Micklesea ahead. This would be her destination for the time being.

She walked on as the sun rose higher; the town was now much closer. She approached a small bridge across the river. The river bank on the side that she had been walking down would continue into the small port town of Harflett. Micklesea was on the other side of the river. Maria crossed the bridge and soon found a footpath which followed a small road leading into Micklesea.

This part of her journey was coming to an end. Looking up as the road began to approach the outskirts, she could see the buildings in the town were now very close.

She paused by the roadside for a brief rest. Then rummaging through her handbag, took out a small rectangular vanity mirror. Her hair was a mess, her sore left cheek was beginning to come out in a bruise. It was now daylight, so reaching into her bag she pulled out some dark glasses and put them on. Although they covered some of the bruise it was still noticeable.

After tidying up her hair, she pressed on. She would try to see if some makeup would help conceal the mark on her cheek once she had arrived in the main town.

It was a little more than an hour later when Maria finally reached the seafront at Micklesea. It was out of season so there were relatively few visitors around. She had stopped for a rest a few times as tiredness crept up on her. Now she spotted a bench on the promenade where she could take a longer breather.

She sat down.

Her sunglasses hid the fact that she was able to take time to catch up on her sleep. But not for too long. She was cat napping. Between times checking her bags, tracking time and staring out to sea deep in thought.

Sometime later she peered at her watch again. She had been sitting down on the bench for over an hour. Although still feeling her aching limbs, she decided to get some refreshment. She had noticed a small café earlier, close to the shore and a little way along the promenade. She resolved it would be an ideal place for a nice cup of tea.

Having made her way to the café, she sat at a small table and ordered a cup of tea, a large muffin and a breakfast roll.

This would keep her going whilst she decided what to do next.

It was a pleasant enough day that followed. Especially considering the trauma of the previous night, but by afternoon Maria was again beginning to turn her thoughts to the future. She sat herself in the sunshine on the sea wall with an ice cream when an idea formulated in her mind.

She had spotted a bus stop on her way to the café earlier. One of the buses that stopped there would take her back to the town she had left last night. The thought of that sent a shiver down her spine. Another bus pulled up. This one terminated at the Harflett ferry port. She checked her bag. Inside it she rummaged around and found her passport. As she looked back towards Harflett she noticed a ferry in dock. She resolved this would be her escape.

The bus had already gone but she had no need to rush. She finished the ice cream and then made her way to the bus stop. The next bus to Harflett was not for forty-five minutes. But she could wait.

When she finally arrived at the ferry port it was much later in the day. The last ferry had departed. But there would be another one in the morning. So, she found a seat and waited for that one. Tomorrow morning would be the start of her new life.

2

It was now almost a year since Maria had left England for the continent. She had now settled into a new life in a small city on the Dutch-Belgian border. Westelburg was a quiet and diverse city. It had enabled Maria to transform into her new persona. She had changed her name and become Jo Newchurch, a name she had originally constructed with a close friend of hers back in England before she had left home.

Jo had settled into her new life working during the day as a waitress in a hotel, where she had also found lodgings. In order to top up her earnings, she would often do other work including behind the bar in the hotel.

As a result of her living and working in the area, she had begun to develop new friendships.

One such friend was Christabella, an attractive woman who also worked in the hotel. Christabella had been raised in Spain and Italy before moving to Westelburg.

They often met up together and on this particular night, they were both seated at a table close to the bar area in the hotel reception. Both were dressed lavishly and had added lots of accessories and make up.

Jo was looking pensive; her mind elsewhere.

'You seem deep in thought, Jo,' Christabella said, staring inquisitively at her friend. Jo nodded. 'Are you unhappy?'

'A little bit.' Jo paused still deep in thought. 'Just thinking back, you know. Thinking about how my life has turned out.'

'You are happy here though?'

'Yeah. Yeah of course. I suppose.'

Christabella took a sip from her drink. 'I'm meeting someone here tonight, Jo.' She smiled uncharacteristically coyly.

'Are you?' Jo had a suspicion what Christabella was referring to but let it pass.

'Yes. I should be able to treat you to lunch tomorrow.'

'Thanks Bella but I'm working tomorrow over lunch.'

'Oh. Maybe another day then?' Christabella returned to her drink.

'Are you feeling flush?'

'What do you mean?'

'Do you have lots of money to spend?'

'I hope so after tonight.'

'Oh OK. Maybe we'll do lunch later in the week then.'

'Yes, Jo. I'd like that.'

There was another long pause. Christabella started eyeing up the people coming into the reception area. Jo began stirring her drink with her straw.

'I am glad I came here, Bella.'

Christabella looked back at Jo. 'Of course, it's nice here.'

'No, I mean I'm glad I came to Westelburg. I really needed to come here.' Christabella listened as Jo continued. 'You know, when I was young, I had dreams. Lots of dreams. I wanted to do things. I wanted to make a difference. I wanted to, maybe, meet a handsome man who would sweep me off my feet. You know what I mean. We'd fall madly in love. Settle down. Maybe. Have a family. You know the sort of thing.' Christabella smiled and laughed quietly. Jo continued her reminiscing. 'When I was at school, I had a dream. I wanted to become a nun. I went to a convent school. Yes, I dreamed of being a nun. I remember I had some nice teachers there. Really supportive. Where did it all go wrong?'

'But you're happy here now though.'

'Yeah. Of course.'

'Jo we're having so much fun. Enjoying life. And making money. Lots of money. This must be so much better than when you were in England.'

Jo nodded somewhat unconvincingly. 'I know. It's crazy. It's just that sometimes I wish I was back in England.'

'Why?'

'Not my previous life. No. I left all that behind. A new life there. Somewhere else.'

'Do you think you are a bit house sick?' Christabella stumbled over the word.

Jo grinned. 'I think you mean homesick, Bella. Yeah maybe.' She sighed.

'I'm sure it will pass, Jo.' Christabella started looking around again. 'Don't worry. You know, I sometimes wonder if I might one day try to get a job in England. Some day.'

Jo looked back to her and smiled. 'Really?'

'Yes. Who knows?' Jo picked up her drink and Christabella shrugged her shoulders playfully. 'I might be able to make even more money there.' She smiled.

Jo laughed too. Then returned to her drink.

'Perhaps we could both find a new life there, Bella.'

'As you said, Jo. Who knows?'

A well-dressed gentleman walked into reception. He was carrying some flowers. He walked over to the reception desk and after a short, seemingly slightly awkward conversation, the receptionist beckoned Christabella over.

'It's my date, Jo,' Christabella said, tipping the rest of her drink back. 'I'll speak to you tomorrow. Wish me luck.'

'Good luck, Bella. Take care. Be careful.'

'Always do, Jo. See you. Ciao.'

'Ciao,'

She flashed a smile back to Jo then turned her attention to the man by the reception desk. She waved and smiled over to him as she walked over. They immediately began a conversation.

Jo watched intently as they spoke. Then smiled as they walked out of the reception area into the bar.

Jo followed a few minutes later and ordered herself another drink. Then, glancing briefly over to the small alcove where Christabella and her man were sitting, she returned to her seat in the reception area.

She began flicking through text messages. Occasionally sipping her drink and looking around as people came and went.

Christabella and her gentleman disappeared to the lifts.

Sometime later the receptionist called over. 'Jo!'

She looked up. He was on the phone. 'What is it?'

'Are you working tonight?'

'No. I'm waitressing tomorrow. The bar is OK tonight.'

'No, I didn't mean on the bar.'

'Oh.' She paused and checked herself over. 'I hadn't intended to. Why do you have something for me?'

'Yes. If you want it.'

'OK.'

'It's a Mr Dupont in room 216. Henri Dupont.'

Jo thought this through and decided why not. 'OK. Tell him I'm on my way up. Say I'll be about fifteen minutes though. I'd better just tidy myself up first.'

'Will do.'

Jo stood up and walked briskly over to the ladies' restroom.

'Thanks,' she called back to the receptionist. 'See you later.'

3

It was a bright sunny day in the city; a typical day in England at the end of the summer. Jo was making her way through the supermarket car park when she was startled by a call from someone nearby.

'Maria!' the voice shouted. 'Hi Maria. It is you, isn't it?'

Jo turned towards the woman. She was casually dressed and carrying a large shopping bag. Jo froze to the spot. She thought the woman looked familiar but couldn't quite place where she knew her from.

'Hi Maria,' the woman repeated as she approached and, seeing the stunned look on Jo's face quickly followed up with, 'It's Lynda. We went to school together. You know. St Josephs.'

Jo stood rooted to the spot. Her mind was racing. She muttered weakly. 'Oh hi Lynda.'

'Imagine bumping into you here. What are you doing? Do you live here?'

'Yes,' Jo said, uncertainly.

'I'm just passing through on holiday. You do look a little different, Maria. A little older.' She chuckled. 'I guess we are all a little older now though, aren't we?'

'Sorry, Lynda.' Jo tried to regain some composure. 'My name is Jo.'

'Really!'

'Yes.'

'Wow. You do look so much like Maria from school.'

'No. I'm definitely Jo.'

'Oh, I'm sorry, Jo. Forgive me. It would have been quite a coincidence though, wouldn't it? As I say, I'm just passing through. You do look so much like her.'

Jo cast her mind back to those schooldays. She remembered she was never particularly close to Lynda at school. They had different groups of friends. Jo was surprised Lynda had recognised her.

As Lynda began to head away, Jo's inquisitiveness got the better of her. 'What was this Maria like then?' Jo asked, immediately regretting continuing a conversation that may well have been coming to a natural end. She wanted to speak to Lynda about her schooldays but she knew it would probably be too dangerous to delve very far.

'Well, she was quite a sweet girl as I remember. I went to a convent school. I didn't really get on with the nuns. Maria did though. She always enjoyed life. She enjoyed so much at school. I never really understood why.'

Jo started to remember that happy, carefree girl back in her schooldays. She smiled back at Lynda. 'Yes. She sounds nice.'

'Well must fly,' Lynda started walking away. 'Sorry about the confusion.'

'Bye, Jo.'

'Yes. Bye, Lynnie.'

Jo looked on as Lynda disappeared into the distance. She saw Lynda get into a car and drive off. Turning back Jo headed off in the other direction towards her home and the flats nearby where she lived.

Lynda had driven some miles before she realised what had been nagging on her mind following the meeting with Jo. Suddenly, it came to her. Jo called her "Lynnie". No one had called her that since her days at the convent school. Perhaps it was Maria after all. She began to wonder why she would have lied.

Back at her ground-floor flat, Jo had arrived still a little unnerved by her encounter with Lynda in the car park. She poured herself a drink and sat down to think back to that schoolgirl Lynda had spoken about. A girl who befriended her teachers, was always well behaved and very respectful and understanding of the religious life that the nuns who taught her had chosen to live.

She sighed. A deep long sigh and began stirring her coffee thoughtfully. Once again, she found herself falling into another one of her contemplative moods.

After a short while her thoughts were interrupted by noises at the front door of the building. Jo walked over to the window. The girls were arriving for the evening. She walked out to the corridor to greet them.

'Hi. Afternoon everyone,' she called cheerily.

They replied with a 'Hi' 'Hi, Jo' or something similarly cheerful.

'It looks like we could be in for a busy night tonight, girls,' Jo said as they passed by.

The girls began to make their way to their respective flats.

'Lots of money to be made then,' one of them responded.

'Yes, Bella. Lots of money.' She laughed. Bella and some of the other girls joined in.

'Oh. By the way, I've been shopping and restocked our cupboards. So, if you need anything for later, it should be there for you. Just help yourselves and let me know if you have any problems.'

Bella walked over to Jo and planted a kiss on her cheek. 'Thanks, Jo. We all love you so much.'

Jo smiled. Bella gently wiped the lipstick mark off of Jo's cheek and headed upstairs to her flat with a wave and a further air kiss.

As the afternoon turned to evening, Jo began receiving callers on the phone and at the main door. She led the callers at the door into the building and directed them to the flat they required.

It was indeed going to be a busy night. Bella and all the girls would be well pleased with their rewards for the night's work.

4

Walking through the convent corridors, Sister Olivia made her way quietly into the Chapel of the Order of St Sabina. At the front of the chapel a new trainee was kneeling and whispering a prayer. As Sister Olivia approached, she could hear her speaking quietly.

'...for I know my transgressions and my sin is always before me. Against you, and you only, have I sinned and done what is evil in your sight. So that you are proved right when...' Maria paused as Olivia settled beside her.

'Sister Olivia,' Maria said.

'Maria, you need not stop. I don't wish to interrupt your prayer.'

Maria returned to her prayer. 'So that you are proved right when you speak and justified when you judge.'

She stopped again. Sister Olivia looked at her.

'Do you wish to speak, Maria?'

Maria thought for a moment. 'Sister I am still troubled. I feel unworthy and searching for answers to my situation.'

Sister Olivia smiled. A caring, friendly smile. 'Once you understand your calling. Once you find your faith you will find your answer.'

Maria looked at Sister Olivia with a pained expression. 'But I am so troubled Sister. I have broken many of the Lord's commandments and committed many sins. I have sold my body for sexual gratification. I have sold others in the same way. I have lied, deceived and earned money immorally. But most of all I have taken the life of someone, my husband, with whom God blessed our union in matrimony.'

'Maria, it is true that you have done many of these things but you did not kill your husband.'

'I know he beat me abused me and...' she trailed off, 'but I still killed him.'

'Maria, your husband died some months after you left him. He was caught up in a brawl outside a bar. He was drunk. The others involved were also drunk. It all turned violent and he was killed then.'

'But...' Maria was stunned. She stared back at Sister Olivia quizzically, 'Is this really true?'

'Yes, Maria. It made many of the national papers. It was whilst you were in Europe.'

Maria sat silently. Then looking back up to Sister Olivia returned to the plight she faced. 'That is some relief, Sister. But nevertheless, how will I be judged for all my other sins? Can I ever find true forgiveness?'

'Maria, we are none of us without sin. You must come to terms with your past and it will help you prepare for your future.'

'I do want my future to be here.'

'We are praying for you, Maria. We believe your future can be with us. You must find your own way. You can do this through your faith.' Sister Olivia paused as Maria began to take in what she had said and yet looked quizzically back at her.

Maria sighed. 'How can you ever have faith in me after what I have done?'

'Reverend Mother has faith in you. I have faith in you. We all have faith in you. You can find your faith. You know you have sinned; you know that who you were then is not who you wish to be in the future. If you learn from your past, you will be able to move forward, discover the real Maria, you can devote yourself to the service of St Sabina and find the faith that you feel you lost for a while. And your sins can be forgiven.'

'Your words are most helpful, Sister Olivia,' Maria replied looking more peaceful. 'I hope I can repay your faith in me. And Reverend Mother's faith taking me in and believing in me.'

Sister Olivia held Maria's hand. 'I am here to help you, Maria. Reverend Mother has given me this task. I will help you find your faith. I am here to help lead you through your doubts and to enable you to achieve the calling that you seek with us.'

'Thank you, Sister.'

Still holding Maria's hand, Sister Olivia continued,

'Reverend Mother shared a story with me from her time when she was a teacher. She told me of a young girl she had met. That young girl was full of youthful exuberance. Just as you would expect of one so young. She also had a curiosity. A curiosity to learn about the gospel, about her teachers and their commitment to the church. Their devotion to the Word of God.'

'Reverend Mother was a teacher?'

'Yes, a teacher. When she came to us it was decided she could best serve others by teaching them and educating them to become better people. It was decided to send her to a school in the area. That school was St Joseph's. And to use her skills so the children could learn the Word of God.'

Maria listened intently.

'At St Sabina's we always believe in giving something back to our community. It is part of our service. We become their servants and their teachers. The young children may learn the joy of our message.' Sister Olivia paused. 'We can hope that one day, one or two of them may join us so we can spread that message further. As we do.'

'Reverend Mother taught at St Joseph's?' Maria mumbled as she slowly processed the information from her colleague. Sister Olivia nodded.

'We know you have suffered, Maria. We also know that you have within you the ability to move forward to better things. Remember how joyful life can be. Understand how you may have been tested and how you can now choose a different way. To serve St Sabina. Maybe you too will find your vocation teaching in the community as Reverend Mother did. To share the word. To use your trials, your ordeals and to help you learn and to teach others to find a better way. You have so many experiences in your past. You also have a future. In that future you may mould yourself into someone who can serve St Sabina and make others better people.'

Maria looked up to the statue of the Saint. 'Sister, I am determined to work hard here. To be the best I can be. I feel I have found my calling. My home. But first I must learn to prove myself to Reverend Mother; to St Sabina.'

'Reverend Mother's story shows you that, in many ways, you have already gone some way down the path to prove your worth to her.'

Maria bowed her head in thought and contemplation.

Sister Olivia continued. 'There is more you can learn from us. That is true. But you should seek to find that youthful girl's faith. An exuberance that you once had and channel it anew to the service of the Saint. We know you are capable of doing this. You must believe in yourself. Once you do this you will learn more about yourself and we will learn more about Maria too.'

'I think I can see that,' Maria said softly and with the merest hint of a smile.

'It is the first step, Maria. Each day we all set out on our personal road. A road to redemption. In your life you will have taken many steps. Sometimes our path becomes confused and we may lose our way. Then we seek the right path again. When you find that path you may find it will lead you to far greater things. Those things that you truly seek. You can then find it much easier to confront your past sins and begin those first steps to a more impressive and fruitful future. To serve. To teach. But in the end, we all continue to learn each and every day. As we learn more about the world, we also learn more about ourselves. Then we can share that knowledge to make the world a better place. A better place for everyone whoever they are and wherever they may seek to find us.

Printed in Great Britain
by Amazon